The Riddle of Greatness

The Song of Roland presents a baffling puzzle. We know neither its date nor its author. All we can be certain of is the historical fact of the battle of Roncesvals in 778 and the literary fact of a bundle of seventy-two small leaves of parchment now in the library of Oxford University. Yet upon these slender foundations towers a supreme example of what scholar and translator Robert Harrison calls "the enigmatic process called epic fermentation, which is somehow able to transform an accident of history into the unique, inevitable expression of a whole people." To read *The Song of Roland* is to enter into the very soul of a gallant, brutal, and tumultuous age.

Robert Harrison was born in Wichita Falls, Texas, in 1932. He received the B.A. degree from the University of Texas in 1953, and following a tour of duty in the United States Navy returned for the M.A. in 1960 and the Ph.D. in 1964. He is the author of books and articles on Beckett, Faulkner, Crashaw, Donne, and Keats, and is the coeditor of *Masterworks of World Literature*. He is also the author of *Gallic Salt: Eighteen Fabliaux translated from the Old French*.

THE SONG
OF
ROLAND

♦

Translated from the Old French
and with an Introduction by
ROBERT HARRISON

A MENTOR BOOK

MENTOR
Published by the Penguin Group
Penguin Books USA Inc., 375 Hudson Street,
New York, New York 10014, U.S.A.
Penguin Books Ltd, 27 Wrights Lane,
London W8 5TZ, England
Penguin Books Australia Ltd, Ringwood,
Victoria, Australia
Penguin Books Canada Ltd, 10 Alcorn Avenue,
Toronto, Ontario, Canada M4V 3B2
Penguin Books (N.Z.) Ltd, 182–190 Wairau Road,
Auckland 10, New Zealand

Penguin Books Ltd, Registered Offices:
Harmondsworth, Middlesex, England

Published by Mentor, an imprint of Dutton Signet,
a division of Penguin Books USA Inc.

First Mentor Printing, August, 1970
18   17   16   15   14   13

 REGISTERED TRADEMARK—MARCA REGISTRADA

Library of Congress Catalog Card Number: 74-124489

Printed in the United States of America

Contents

INTRODUCTION

I

The *Song of Roland* presents one of the most baffling puzzles in the history of French literature. None of the poem's "vital statistics"—its date, its author, its sources—have been established conclusively, and although scholars have labored long and hard over these problems, their solution remains as remote today as it was half a century ago.

Deeper still, the poem poses another, even more tantalizing riddle which concerns the nature of epic poetry itself. Over three hundred years separate the hard, clear facts in the case of this the greatest and possibly the oldest *chanson de geste*. At one end there is the historical fact of the battle of Roncesvals on the afternoon of August 15, 778; at the other the literary fact, a bundle of seventy-two small leaves of mediocre-quality parchment catalogued under the name of Digby 23 in the Bodleian Library at Oxford University—and between the two that enigmatic process called epic fermentation, which is somehow able to transform an accident of history into the unique, inevitable expression of a whole people.

The events which make up the historical basis of the story are documented in the colorless Latin prose of Einhard, Charlemagne's contemporary biographer:

> While the war with the Saxons was being fought incessantly and almost continuously, he [Charlemagne] stationed garrisons at suitable places along the frontier and attacked Spain with the largest military force he could muster; he crossed the Pyrenees, accepted the surrender of all the towns and fortresses he attacked, and returned with his army safe and sound, except that he experienced a minor setback caused by Gascon treachery on returning through the passes of the Pyrenees. For while his army was stretched out in a long column, as the terrain and the narrow defiles dictated, the Gascons set an ambush above them on the mountaintops—an ideal spot for an ambush, due to the dense woods throughout the area—and rushing down into the valley, fell upon the end of the baggage train and the rearguard who served as protection for those in advance, and in the ensuing battle killed them to the last man, then seized the baggage, and under the cover of night, which was already falling, dispersed as quickly as possible. The Gascons were aided in this feat by the lightness of their armor and by the lay of the land where the action took place, whereas the Franks were hindered greatly by their heavy armor and the terrain. In this battle Eggihard, the surveyor of the royal table; Anselm, the count of the palace; and Roland, prefect of the Breton Marches, were killed, together with many others. Nor could revenge be taken at the moment, for as soon as the act had been done, the enemy scattered so completely that no trace of them was left behind.[1]

For many years it was supposed that Einhard's report was the only detailed account of the massacre at Roncesvals; but in the 1950's another document, the *Nota Emilianense*, was found in Spain by a scholar named Dámaso Alonso. Written in a Visigothic script and probably dating from the tenth century, it adds yet more texture to the historical fabric of the poem:

> In the year 778 King Charles came to Saragossa; at that time he had twelve nephews [or grandsons?] with him, and each of them had three thousand armed horsemen with him; among them were Roland, Bertrand, Ogier

of the Short Sword, Guillaume of the Hooked Nose . . .
Olivier, and the bishop Turpin. Each one, with his followers, served the king one month of each year. It so happened that the king stopped at Saragossa with his army.
After a short time he was counseled by his men to accept
a number of gifts so that the army might not perish from
hunger and could return to their homeland. This was
done. The king then decided that, for the safety of the
men of the army, the courageous warrior Roland should
remain with the rear guard. But when the army traversed
the Port of Cize, at Roncevaux, Roland was killed by the
Saracens.[2]

These two early accounts would seem to treat the battle
at Roncesvals as little more than a minor setback briefly
clouding the military glory of Charles, but there is reason
to suspect in them some official soft-pedaling of the facts.
Actually, it is quite possible that the defeat at Roncesvals
was an almost catastrophic blow to the Carolingian empire
and that, therefore, its selection as subject matter for a
chanson de geste is not so far-fetched as the contemporary
reports might lead one to believe.

Relations between Moslem Spain and Christian France
were as devious and involved as medieval diplomacy could
be and usually was. Ever since the days of Charlemagne's
grandfather, Charles Martel, there had been a constant
threat from the south, not only from the Arabs who had
occupied the ancient region of Septimania in southern
France, but also from the separatist Christian dukes of
Aquitaine, Narbonne, and Provence. For this reason, his
celebrated crusade which stopped the northward advance
of the Saracens also included a less-publicized punitive
expedition against the rebellious Christians of the Midi.
His successor, Pepin the Short, recaptured Septimania
(752–59), thanks partly to the internal squabbling of the
two rival Moslem factions within Spain, the Abbasids and
the Omayyads. Then, in a neat bit of political maneuver-
ing, the Abbasid governor of Barcelona, Suleiman, placed
himself under the nominal protection of Pepin in order to
weaken his Omayyad enemy, Abdur Rahman. This opened
the door for Frankish military intervention, but Pepin died
soon afterwards, and an expedition to Spain would have
to await the leisure of his son, Charles.

Several years went by before Charles was able to con-solidate his position in the north sufficiently to do anything about Spain. But by 777, when a delegation of Arabs led by Suleiman showed up in Paderborn and offered him a piece of northern Spain in exchange for aid against Abdur Rahman, the time seemed ripe to combine the business of territorial expansion with the pleasure of crusading. To these ends he assembled a huge levy of troops (though nothing like the 350,000 given him by the *Song of Roland*) and headed south.

Dividing his army into two columns, Charles executed a pincers maneuver on Saragossa: the western column pushed down through the Pyrenees to the Christian city of Pam-plona, overran it despite the bitter resistance put up by its Gascon inhabitants, then joined Suleiman and the hostages he offered as proof of his fidelity, and marched southeast-ward on Saragossa. Meanwhile the eastern column moved through Septimania and down the east coast of Spain to Barcelona, where they turned westward toward Saragossa.

So far the expedition had been an unqualified success; but once at Saragossa, Charles's troubles began. A rebel friend of Suleiman's named Al-Husein suddenly took the city himself and refused to hand it over to the Franks. Then, after a month of fruitless efforts to dislodge him, Charles got word that his old enemies the Saxons were up in arms again. Reluctantly lifting his siege, he headed back toward France, taking with him many hostages including Suleiman himself, whom he now suspected of double-crossing him.

On the way home the entire Frankish force withdrew along the western route, and once again the Gascons of Pamplona gave their fellow Christians an unfriendly re-ception. Out of patience with them, Charles destroyed their city. But they were to have the last laugh: conspiring with an unknown number of Arabs, the Pamplonians set the ambush at Roncesvals and got away unharmed. The par-ticipation of Moslem forces at the battle, a subject care-fully omitted by both Einhard and the author of the *Nota Emilianense,* is nonetheless strongly argued by the state-ment of an historian from the other side, ibn-al-Athir, who simply says that the sons of Suleiman were successful in liberating their father from the Franks.

At this point history leaves off and speculation begins. Ever since the first printed edition of the *Song of Roland* appeared in 1837, literary historians have argued tirelessly over how and why this particular battle should have become the inspiration for France's first great work of literature.[8] By and large, scholars have drawn up their battle lines according to Romantic or Classical sympathies. The nineteenth-century medievalist Gaston Paris, for example, took as his point of departure a fashionable theory which held the *Iliad* and the *Odyssey* to be descended from folklore. He maintained that the *Song of Roland* was the product of a new sense of national identity emergent among the French people at the time of the First Crusade, and that its immediate origin was to be found in short folk songs called *cantilènes* which had grown up around the Roncesvals theme through centuries of epic fermentation, finally to appear, in a late, almost decadent stage, as the *Song of Roland.* Then, in the early years of the twentieth century, anti-Romantic reaction set in, championed by Joseph Bédier, who refused to accept the poem as a folk-creation and proclaimed it to be the work of a single individual of great artistic genius. According to Bédier, the story of Roncesvals had survived in the form of oral legends circulated along the pilgrimage routes of Europe, especially those of northern Spain. The road to the famous shrine of Saint James at Compostella, for instance, led through the pass of Roncesvals itself; all along this road there were hostels for pilgrims, and at these hostels monks who kept alive the names of local Christian heroes and their great deeds until, finally, spurred by the Crusading fever of the eleventh century, their tales were set down on paper by traveling poets called *jongleurs,* and the gap between folklore and literature was bridged. Finally the poet, working from the songs of the *jongleurs,* created the poem we know as the *Song of Roland.* Fairly recently, an eminent Spanish literary historian, R. Menéndez Pidal, has modified Bédier's view somewhat by proposing a traditionalist explanation which sees the poem as the final integer in a long and varied sequence of lost works on the Roncesvals theme.

Although these theories seem at first glance quite divergent, they all possess at least one common element: they assume the necessity of an earlier version of the *Song of Roland*. But even within this area of agreement controversies again start to arise concerning the nature and source of the hypothetical proto-*Roland*. Some scholars think it must have been a spoken legend or folktale, while others see it as a full-fledged literary work written in Latin or Provençal or French and originating in southern France or northern France or even in Norman England. It has been argued that it must have been written in the early years of the twelfth century as a propaganda piece intended to warm up tepid Christian interest in the Crusade and at the same time to praise the dashing hero of Antioch, Bohemond; that it is based on military campaigns carried out by the Franks against Spain in the second decade of the twelfth century and celebrates specifically the capture of Saragossa in 1118; that it was written at the command of Pope Calixtus II, in order to stir the French to action against the Spanish Moors; and even that certain geographical names in the poem, when properly deciphered, show it was composed about 1085 in an effort to obtain Christian reinforcements for Robert Guiscard, who was campaigning at the time against the Byzantine Greeks in Dalmatia. And so the debate goes on.

It seems doubtful that historians will ever reach agreement on the genesis of the poem, but there is a way for the general reader to avoid this impasse, and that is simply to look at the poem itself. For though scholars may engage in endless debate over *fermentation épique* or the *cantilène* theory, one fact remains which vitiates their point of view: they treat the poem as a mine to be worked for the historical data it yields. In the long run, it is not the lack of factual knowledge which creates the riddle of the *Song of Roland* so much as it is that habit of mind which, regarding a work of art as nothing more than the sum of its raw materials, considers form and structure and theme and style as elements to be extracted, isolated, and put to nonliterary uses. But if we choose to treat the *Song of Roland* as what it is—a unique aesthetic creation—then many scholarly problems become less compelling. Thus armed, we can now graciously entertain the likelihood that folksongs were composed about Roland and Charles, that the Franks seethed, both individually and collectively, with epic fermentation from 778 onwards, or that lesser poets composed proto-*Rolands* by the score—as long as it is understood that what we call the *Song of Roland* exists only as a work of art justifiable for its own sake. And with this in mind, the reader can defend himself against the insidious influence of centrifugal arguments such as this: "The proto-*Roland* must have been written before the twelfth century, because there is in it no hint of courtly love, and love is still regarded simply as the feudal duty of woman." Whether this assertion is true or not, it contributes nothing to our knowledge of the poem and is therefore of no literary significance—we already knew from a close reading that the poem contained no elements of courtly love.[4]

Another benefit to be gained from reading the poem as literature concerns the question of its unity. Many early critics, dedicated to seeing the poem solely as a piece of historical documentation, insisted that the entire Baligant episode and the embassy of Blancandrin were late interpolations, and therefore ought to be stricken from the "real" text. Though it is true that these episodes have been omitted wholly or in part from at least one Old Norse and two Latin versions of the poem, the overriding fact is that they are indisputably *there* in the Oxford manuscript and in all other Old French texts.

With these caveats in mind, we may now return to the historical background of the poem and examine it briefly from a literary point of view. All speculation as to date aside, the facts are these: (1) There is no direct reference to the Crusades anywhere in the poem, and hence no absolute need to date it after 1096. (2) Around the end of the eleventh century, hints of the existence of a poem celebrating Roland begin to appear. (3) William of Malmesbury, writing about 1125, says that just before the battle of Hastings a minstrel sang to William the Conqueror's troops of Roland, "so that the warlike example of the hero would enflame those who were about to fight." Taking these facts into account, we might as well assume that the *Song of Roland* was written sometime around the beginning of the twelfth century.

Of more immediate interest, however, is the way history and legend are used in the poem. Obviously a skillful, talented writer has shaped from the conglomerate of history, religion, folklore, and earlier literature a compact, highly unified work of art. Take for instance the treachery of the Saracens. An historical precedent can be found in Einhard's description of the Saxon wars:

> It [the war] might have been over earlier, had the perfidy of the Saxons been exposed. It is difficult to say how often they conceded defeat and offered themselves to the king as suppliants, promised to obey his orders, handed over the required hostages without delay, and received the envoys who were sent forth; how frequently they, so cowed and submissive, swore to give up their worship of devils and to yield themselves to the Christian religion. But even though they were often prone to do these things, they were always prompt to renege, so that it is impossible to say which course they followed more readily, for from the beginning of the war there was hardly a year in which they did not both promise and fail to perform.[5]

This passage need not be read as proof of a direct line of influence from Einhard to the author of the *Song of Roland,* but rather as some indication of the poet's technical skill. Here he has grafted an historical detail of the Saxon war onto the Spanish campaign in order to create an aura of verisimilitude which will lend credence to the necessary fictions of his plot, such as Ganelon's betrayal and the selection of an ambassador to Marsilla.

Another interesting use of an historical source may be found in the stormy relations of France and Spain during the eleventh century. At the beginning of the century Christian power had once again deteriorated in the north of Spain: the shrine of Saint James had been desecrated and plundered, and the Moslems had recaptured Barcelona and moved across the Pyrenees. As the century wore on, however, the French made a concerted effort to push the Moors back, chiefly because of pressure exerted by the zealously Christian wife of King Alphonso VI of Castile. Thanks to her religious fervor, many monasteries were established in northern Spain, and the entire region came back into the European sphere of influence. But this resurgence of militant Christianity so disturbed the Moorish chieftain Yûsuf of Marrakech that he attacked Alphonso and defeated him decisively at the battle of Zalaca in 1086.

At this point the lines of history and epic intersect. According to the *Song of Roland,* there were three separate pagan assaults at Roncesvals: first, Marsilla's nephew Aëlroth led an attack and was beaten back rather easily; next, Marsilla himself advanced with the main body of Saracens, and was repulsed when Roland managed to cut off his hand, but only at the expense of nearly all the Frankish knights; and finally, the rear guard was overrun by a wild charge of 50,000 Negro troops under the command of the caliph. Similarly, at the battle of Zalaca a vanguard of Andalusian Arabs made the initial attack on Alphonso, while Yûsuf remained concealed in the hills; when Alphonso succccded in driving back the Arabs, the main force under Yûsuf attacked. The outcome of the battle hung in the balance for a while, until the pagans werc reinforced by a contingent of ferocious Negro guards, and the Christians were routed. At some time during the engagement King Alphonso was wounded in the hand.

Here it would seem that history is being made to serve a literary purpose, but once again it must be stressed that the end-product is our primary conccrn. The loss of a hand, for instancê: an adventitious detail at the battle of Zalaca, in the *Song of Roland* it acquires the sort of representational value that we normally associate with symbolism, and becomes much more significant than its literal meaning could possibly warrant. By helping to maintain a scrupulous balance in the military fortunes of the Saracens and the Franks, it contributes to the reader's awareness that there is more at stake at Roncesvals than just another battle, that there is present here an element history usually lacks—*form.* As one critic has observed, "Roland, who has been depicted as the perfect knight, could not go to his death without first taking his revenge. Had he depended on Charlemagne to even the score, he could hardly be judged perfect by knightly standards. But had he slain Marsile the score would have been far from even, because they were not of equal rank. So he deprived Marsile of exactly the same thing that the Moor was taking from Charlemagne."[6]

In addition, Roland's act has judicial overtones. Mutilation by cutting off the right hand was an accepted punishment for especially heinous criminals, and Roland both symbolically and literally strips Marsilla of his power as a lord and as a man, by rendering him incapable of defending not only his weapons in battle, but his fiefs and chattels as well. By allowing Roland to disgrace him in this way and drive him from the field alive, Marsilla subjects himself to the basest form of humiliation in the eyes of his vassals and his wife. Nor were the subtle social and psychological implications of the act lost on the medieval audience: upon the lintel of the church at Angoulême the sculptor represents with fine ambiguity the retreating figure of Marsilla twisting his body at the last instant to defend himself against Roland.

In the opinion of many scholars, including the German Walter Tavernier, many of the episodes in the *Song of Roland* grew out of the events of the astonishingly successful First Crusade into Syria and Palestine (1096–1108). These similarities have been used chiefly to date the poem or to identify its hero with this or that historical figure, but the same data may be applied just as well to literary ends. Although there are close resemblances in subject matter, style, and tone to the early Latin chronicles of the First Crusade, we need not go along with Tavernier and regard the poem merely as a double-barreled propaganda blast directed at the pagan perils in both the Middle East and Spain. The giant Falsaron may owe his existence to the tale of a giant Saracen killed at the siege of Antioch in 1098; the incident of the pagan standard (v. 3546) may have been inspired by a similar feat of arms which took place at the battle of Ascalon; and it is quite likely that Turpin's militant theology would have been considered heretical prior to the famous Clermont sermon of Pope Urban II—but interesting as these details are in themselves, and convincing as they may be in arguing for a date after 1100, their importance to the reader lies in what the poet has made of them. This sort of question is more to the point: Why is Falsaron the second pagan killed, and the first killed by Olivier? What use does the author make of the pagan standards? What effect does the character of the archbishop have on the theme and structure of the poem?

In the same way that historical incidents are used in the dating game, so echoes from earlier works of literature are often regarded as veiled hints of the identity of the poet.

Yet these same literary influences, when pointed in the proper direction, can shed relevant light on the making of the poem. Take, for instance, the faint echoes of Vergil's *Aeneid*. At the beginning of both poems, the heroes have just completed seven-year campaigns; in both poems envoys are depicted carrying olive branches as tokens of peace, a custom unknown in northern Europe, where the olive tree does not grow; then there is Baligant's mighty spear, which may have been modeled on that of Goliath's brother Lachmi, "whose spear staff was like a weaver's beam," (I Chron. 20) but may equally well descend from Aeneas's spear, which was "huge as a tree" (XII:887); and, finally, the savage form of punishment meted out to Ganelon, which is found neither in Germanic tradition nor the Carolingian law codes, but has a literary precedent in the execution of the traitor Mettus (VIII).

Once again literary considerations should come first. The seven-year campaign—seven years being in the Middle Ages proverbial for a great duration—sets the stage for the widespread disaffection and willingness to compromise in the Frankish camp which will put in motion the machinery of betrayal. The olive branches borne by the pagan messengers, by parodying the practices of antiquity, add the element of travesty to treason. More significant than the literary antecedents of Baligant's spear is its symbolic function; its name, *Maltet,* which probably means "Evil," suggests that it stands for the whole, vast power of the pagan world, locked in deadly struggle with Christendom, here imaged by Charles's sword *Joyeuse.* Even the death of Ganelon is important not because it perpetuates a classical literary tradition, but because it represents a form of retribution peculiarly fitting to the nature of his offense.

Perhaps the most baffling riddle of all appears in the last line of the poem: *Ci falt la geste que Turoldus declinet.* Ambiguous in almost every word, this line may serve as a paradigm of the magnitude of scholarly ignorance. Is the *geste* referred to this poem, or the lost proto-*Roland,* or is it merely an unknown chronicle the poet used as his source? Does *declinet* mean "compose," "copy down," or, as some have ventured, "grow weak"? And above all, who is this shadowy figure named Turoldus—clerk or *jongleur,* poet or scribe?

As one might anticipate, vast amounts of energy and ingenuity have been expended in hunting down eleventh-century Frenchmen named Turoldus and linking them to the *Song of Roland*. Internal evidence throughout the poem suggests that the author was a well-educated clergyman who had some precise, though limited, geographical knowledge of northern Spain, and was familiar with the Bible, the *Aeneid*, and the Latin histories of the Franks. In addition, his name, a variant of the Scandinavian *Thorvaldr*, indicates that he may have been a Norman. The most likely candidate in the Turoldus sweepstakes nowadays is a monk from Fécamp who fought at Hastings, served as abbot at Malmesbury and at Peterborough, and died in 1098. It must be kept in mind, however, that all this speculation rests ultimately upon one single line which bristles with ambiguities, and that there is not a shred of genuine evidence to connect any historical personage with the poem. So until such time as proof may come to light, we are justified in identifying Turoldus only in the manner that we identify Homer—as the man who wrote the poem.

One other scholarly puzzle ought to be mentioned briefly here—the mysterious "AOI." This cryptic signature, most often written in capital letters but sometimes "Aoi" and "aoi" as well, occurs 172 times throughout the poem: 158 times at the end of verse paragraphs, and 14 times in other locations. No other manuscript in the Old French language has anything like it, and none of the later medieval translators of the *Song of Roland* show any indication that they understand its purpose. In the early days of *Roland* scholarship it was rather casually assumed to be a battle cry or possibly a *jongleur*'s private key to abridgement, but more recently scholars have tended to identify it as a vocalise, an exercise for singers, based probably on the Latin phrase P(A)X V(O)B(I)SCUM, P(A)X D(O)M(I)NI, "peace be with you, peace of the Lord." This interpretation suggests that it might have been a musical notation signaling either the uninflected monotone used in some liturgical chants, or perhaps a sustained final vowel sound to mark a close.

But the explanations of AOI only begin here—in the last few years it has been identified as the surviving vestige of an ancient refrain related to the *alleluia*, as a short form of the French (A)INSI S(O)IT (I)L, "so be it," and, most ingeniously, as not AOI at all, but as the scribe's misreading of *Am.,* the standard abbreviation of Amen.

Despite all these theories, there are a few things we may safely say about the elusive AOI. First of all, its function is unquestionably aesthetic—it is almost invariably found at the end of verse paragraphs, where form and rhetorical structure crest simultaneously, and it normally accompanies a shift of scene or of atmosphere. (As a matter of fact, even when AOI is missing from the end of a paragraph, about half the time it follows the first line of the next, suggesting that the scribe may simply have misplaced it through carelessness.) And finally, from a literary point of view, all these varying interpretations amount to about the same thing—whether AOI meant to the poet "so be it" or "*alleluia*" or "Amen," it signals to the reader a moment of heightened significance in the action.

II

In *Raoul de Cambrai,* a twelfth-century *chanson de geste,* the hero, who has spent a busy day burning down a convent full of nuns, comes home and orders meat to be served at supper. His knights are appalled by this request. "Today is Good Friday!" they remind him indignantly. "Do you want to slay our souls?"

This incident, exaggerated as it is, may serve to point up the narrowly literal attitude toward religion characteristic of the early Middle Ages. To the medieval nobleman piety meant a familiar, almost intimate relationship to the human natures of Jesus, Mary, and the saints of the church, and included not only what we think of as religious devotion, but also unswerving loyalty, national pride, chivalric honor, and a fierce sense of personal dignity. In those days Western Christianity had very little in common with the philosophical otherworldliness of the Eastern Church. In fact, it was so unabashedly linked to the mundane and the material that during the Crusades the Byzantine Greeks often suspected their Roman Catholic allies of idolatry. For in spite of the Cluniac reforms of the tenth century, the Frankish knight regarded his obligations to God in very much the same terms as his allegiance to his feudal over-lord. But unsophisticated as the faith of the average man may have been, it was nevertheless wholly sincere and zealously militant. It was, in fact, precisely what has since come to be known as the "crusading spirit," that outlook which led eleventh-century Europeans to leave their homes and embark upon a grandiose, idealistic quest in the Holy Land. In the eyes of medieval Christians all non-Christians were despicable worshipers of graven images and false gods, but if awards were to be handed out for heresy, then the nod would have gone to the Moslems. Of course, idolatry has always been specifically forbidden to Moslems, but the Europeans did not know this, and it was a common-place among Roman Catholics to see them as fanatical fetishists, and to associate Islam in a vague way with pre-Christian paganism. As a matter of fact, knowledge of the Moslems at the time of the *Song of Roland* was still so meager that the Saracens depicted in the poem look less like individuals than hideous imitations of the Christian knights they oppose in battle, and their religion seems to be little more than an obscene parody of medieval Catholi-cism. The Saracens, like the Franks, have their "trinity" of Apollo, Mohammed, and Termagant (a distant ancestor of Shakespeare's devil Termagant in *Hamlet*), who are represented in the poem as idols alternately worshiped and vilified by the pagans, depending on the fortunes of war.

Even the faint glimpses of Islamic history and culture which appear occasionally in the poem tend to reveal the poet's ignorance rather than his knowledge. The titles given the various pagan champions, for instance, make up a pot-pourri from four centuries of Arab history: the agnomen *al khalifah,* "successor" (to Mohammed), was in use until the eleventh century; *almodaffer,* "victorious," was the surname of Hakam, a king of Cordova in Charlemagne's time; and *al mansûr,* "victorious," had belonged to the tenth-century Arab hero Mohammed ibn-Ali-Abir, whose fifty-six campaigns against the Europeans apparently had not been completely forgotten even by the time of the *Song of Roland.* Evidently the poet was trying to furnish a bit of the exotic local color his countrymen associated with Spain and Islam, while at the same time describing the Moslem world in a fashion both comprehensible to his audience and suitable to the allegorical needs of the poem. Thus the balancing of forces at Roncesvals serves not only to build up the tension finally released in Charlemagne's magnificent single combat with the emir, but it also provides the Saracens with twelve peers to match those of France.

Beneath these surface details lies the unspoken assumption that the pagan world was a mirror-image of the Christian, structured in exactly the same manner yet inverted in every particular. This attitude is revealed by an occasional offhand remark by the poet—when describing an especially valorous Saracen, for example, he says with open admiration that he would have been an ideal chevalier, had he only been a Christian. By the same token, when Roland dies he freely offers his soul to the archangels, while Marsilla's is wrested from him by "lively devils." Nor is this attitude to be found solely in literature: on the west façade of the church at Conques, in southern France, Christ is represented with his right hand raised in a gesture signifying truth, while Satan extends his left hand downward.

Even in the specialized business of waging war, both the Franks and the Saracens seem to observe identical customs. Battles are formally announced by heralds; warriors request their commanders to give them the honor of opening a battle by striking the first blow; knights announce their presence and intentions to the enemy by means of formal boasts; and both sides make use of traditional battle cries to keep up their fighting spirit and to rally their units.[7] In addition, both the Christians and the Saracens carry battle standards or ensigns; here Charles's *oriflamme,* the golden banner of the city of Rome, which, by the way, was actually presented to Charlemagne by Pope Leo III—though years after Roncesvals—is pitted symbolically against Marsilla's dragon and the ensigns of Baligant. It should be made clear that these insignia were not as yet heraldic; what we call heraldry, with its elaborate and systematic representation of family alliances, did not develop until long after the time of the *Song of Roland.* In the early Middle Ages knights embellished their shields and carried banners chiefly for identification in the thick of battle when they might easily be mistaken for the enemy. Marsilla's standard should be thought of as much like the one King

Harold displayed at the battle of Hastings—a small wooden or metal effigy fixed on a tall pole and carried by a foot-soldier.

In his life of Charlemagne, the Monk of St. Gall writes:

> Then could be seen the Iron Charles, helmed with an iron helm, his iron breast and his broad shoulders defended by an iron breastplate, an iron spear raised in his left hand, his right always rested on his unconquered iron falchion. The thighs, which with most men are uncovered that they may the more easily ride on horseback, were in his case clad with plates of iron: I need make no special mention of his greaves, for the greaves of all the army were of iron. His shield was of iron, his charger iron-coloured and iron-hearted. The fields and open places were filled with iron, a people stronger than iron paid universal homage to the strength of iron. The horror of the dungeon seemed less than the bright gleam of the iron. "Oh the iron, woe for the iron," was the cry of the citizens. The strong walls shook at the sight of iron, the resolution of old and young fell before the iron.[8]

Though the monk may have been carried away somewhat by his imagery, there is nonetheless a measure of truth in what he says. For Carolingian society, as we see it in the *Song of Roland,* was based on a primitive, unsophisticated form of feudalism not greatly different from the clan society of *Beowulf* and the Old Norse sagas. The division of labor was a simple one: men were classed as warriors or clerics or laborers, and complicating influences such as courtly love had not yet come along to disturb the simple vertical pattern of loyalties which constituted the rationale of social behavior among members of different station. Incidentally, this clear-cut division of labor may help explain why foot-soldiers are practically never mentioned in the poem, even though it was a common practice for feudal lords to require military service from their workers, and Charlemagne's expeditionary force in Spain must have included many thousands of them. The *Song of Roland* was intended to present an idealized portrait of warfare, not a realistic one, and any reminder that there were conscripted, nonprofessional troops at Roncesvals would have struck a jarring note.

At the apex of France's pyramidal society stood the emperor. As commander in chief he placed upon his great lords specific military obligations commensurate with their wealth and power; they in turn demanded the same of their subordinates, and so on, down the line of command. Since the nobility all belonged to the military caste, even the humblest fief-holder physically able to take part in a campaign was expected to contribute his services and provide the personal servants—cooks, grooms, foragers, and the like—necessary to maintain him in the field. Thus the Saracens are wrong to speak of Charles's men as "mercenaries." Although there were some mercenary soldiers by the eleventh century, such as the Varangian Guard of the Byzantine emperors, they were unknown in Charlemagne's time, and the very nature of the feudal system made it necessary for every knight to support himself, with only occasional booty to hope for as his reward.

Charlemagne's army was composed not only of vassal lords and their retainers, but included also many men who held no fief and were bound to the person of their overlords. These landless knights who made up the household guard, or *maisnee,* of a great lord, were often taken into his home as children, given training, sustenance, and armament in return for personal allegiance as well as the customary feudal obligations. The members of a *maisnee* were required by oath to fight to the death for their lord; for this reason, it was important for him to lead his men into battle, and to remain alive and in full view of them, so they would know they were still held to their oaths. If a lord was killed or unhorsed, his followers would be likely to interpret their duties as fulfilled, and head for home. This state of affairs may help explain the emphasis placed on single combats throughout the poem—each chieftain in effect represents a sizable contingent of men ready to fight for him just as long as he is successful, but no longer. Thus the entire pagan host, regarded as Marsilla's *maisnee,* deserts the field of battle the moment Roland puts their lord *hors de combat,* and the same thing happens later when Charles kills Baligant.

In the absence of written law it is in the nature of things

that men will set great store by symbolic gesture. In the rigidly formal social order of medieval France, the assignment of a fief or an honor was invariably accompanied by a ceremonial transfer of tokens, such as a clod of turf or a staff. But perhaps the most universally recognized emblem of all was the glove, symbolic of personal allegiance; when the dying Roland proffers his right-hand glove to God, he is performing the gesture by which a vassal submitted himself to his lord's rule. Later on, Thierry pledges his faith to Charles in precisely the same manner. Similarly, clasping the hands together, an act which made the suppliant momentarily defenseless, had both religious and feudal connotations of voluntary subservience. And when Charlemagne blesses his knights with an upraised right hand, he imitates not only the usual benediction of the Lord, but at the same time recalls that mysterious force the Germanic tribes called *heil*, which was believed to bring success and health.

As a man's duties to his heavenly and earthly lords were delineated with hair-splitting exactness, so were his responsibilities to his family and himself. In the feudal world honor was a family concern; the relatives who pledged themselves for Ganelon, and Pinabel, who put his life on the line for him, were doing no more than what was expected of Christian noblemen. The Saracens, on the other hand, reveal their base natures when they use their own sons as pawns in the treacherous game against Roland.

Relations between social equals were defined with like precision by the Franks. The term "companion," for example, is used throughout the *Song of Roland* to designate either a fellow member of one's *maisnee* or, by extension, a member of one's military unit. The twenty thousand Franks in the rear guard thus become companions by virtue of their assignment, while Roland and Olivier were already companions, since both belonged to the king's *maisnee*. Quite different from the companion was the "friend": though companions were often friends as well, the two terms do not overlap in meaning, for friendship was restricted to personal rather than feudal relationships. Two men of equal station might be bound informally to one another in friendship, and a liege-lord might well call a member of his *maisnee* "friend," but under no circumstances would a vassal use the word in addressing his lord.

Social anthropologists have described Roland's world as a "shame" society; that is, one in which moral attitudes and patterns of behavior are based upon the opinions of other people. As evidence they frequently cite the speech Roland makes to his men, when he reminds them that if they do not fight bravely their names will be held up to public ridicule in mocking songs. This, they argue, explains Roland's reluctance to call for help though hopelessly outnumbered, his final walk across the battlefield toward Spain, and, for that matter, the entire ethos of the poem. It is equally possible, however, that an acute sense of personal honor—what one thinks of oneself—gives rise to the idea of shame. Once again it is the question of the chicken or the egg: does Roland behave heroically because he fears the scorn of his countrymen, or because he would share that scorn himself?

Perhaps the better course is to describe it as a "success" society. Inherent in the medieval world-view is the unquestioned assumption that all is for the best, that in the long run truth and justice are bound to prevail in a world created by an all-powerful, benevolent God. In terms of this dictum, success and failure become the modes of good and evil: that is, whatever succeeds is necessarily right, and whatever fails is wrong. This viewpoint so pervades the *Song of Roland* that even the pagans share it; interpreting their defeat on the battlefield as a total default of their religion, they renounce their gods and desecrate their images. And, *mutatis mutandis,* the Franks, seeing one of their number overwhelm his Saracen opponent, shout jubilantly, "We are in the right and they are in the wrong!"

This pragmatic view of things produces several interesting corollaries. For instance, in a success society there can be no such thing as a "good loser"—the terms contradict one another—and the very fact of defeat imposes a terrible burden of shame upon a knight, his family, and his followers. The language of the poem clearly reflects all this: a common word of abuse such as *caitif,* from the Latin *captivus,* "prisoner," indicates the attitude toward failure, for to be taken alive was a sign of great humiliation, and even to lose one's weapons in the field was cause for reproach.

On the other hand, many of the conventions we associate with honorable behavior seem to be flagrantly disregarded by the Franks. There is no need to look for the modern concept of "fair play" in the single combats of the poem: in a success society sacrificing one's advantage to an enemy is tantamount to disdaining the special favor of God. Though it was considered shameful to attack a foe from behind, this was not due to any obligations to sportsmanship, but simply because a sneak attack could be construed as a tacit acknowledgment of one's inferiority or cowardice. Since a chief goal in battle was to enhance the fame of oneself and one's family, any act that would lessen that fame naturally was to be avoided. Similarly, lines such as "A hundred thousand Franks fall down unconscious" (v. 2932) may strike the modern reader as strangely out of place in a story of valiant deeds and dauntless knights. But the stoical acceptance of misfortune which we expect of our heroes grows out of Germanic paganism, and would have been regarded with contempt in medieval France as evidence of a callous, un-Christian nature. Time and again the Franks weep unashamedly, and in moments of great distress even Charlemagne tears wildly at his beard; but reactions such as these, far from diminishing a man's heroism, were taken as evidence of that quality from which heroism derives its significance: sensibility. The greatness of a man's soul was measured largely by his capacity for suffering, and the stiff upper lip would have been interpreted as proof of either brutishness or stupidity.

But perhaps the most anomalous attitude to be found in the poem is the unreserved adulation of riches and the rich man. The Saracens, of course, are the most notorious offenders in this practice, but the Franks, too, in a most un-Christian fashion, often equate virtue with material wealth. Here again, moral conclusions are determined by the psychology of success. Although the word *riche* overlaps in meaning both *Reich,* "realm," and *rex,* "ruler," and in its original sense refers to power rather than to riches, the idea underlying it is still the same—the man who has right on his side succeeds in every way. The wistful lament, "It might have been," has neither force nor meaning to the characters of the *Song of Roland,* for it implies a flawed universe and hence an imperfect Creator, a conclusion unacceptable to them. The Bildads of the medieval world prevailed.

Many of the elemental moral precepts which shaped Frankish society are brought to the surface by the trial of the traitor Ganelon. At first the proceedings seem to bear a close resemblance to contemporary trial or, more accurately, court-martial procedure. The king, representing himself and the state he rules, is both the offended party and the convening authority. He summons the *seniores,* the wisest men in his realm, and orders them to serve as judges in the case of the Empire v. Ganelon. This done, he steps down to become from now on merely the plaintiff, and neither presides over the court nor dispenses justice himself. Thus the king has voluntarily relinquished the juridical arm of his authority and bound himself to the verdict of the court, leaving the defendant to be tried by a jury of his peers. It is now entirely up to the *seniores* to decide upon the proper course of action: whether Ganelon should be acquitted of the charges against him, or whether he must pay a penalty commensurate with his offense. Since the grave charge of treason has been made, the death sentence would be mandatory in case of conviction.

Up to now Frankish trial procedure looks very much like our own, but here the resemblances end. It soon becomes apparent that the trial of Ganelon is not what we call a trial, but is rather an appeal. The court makes no attempt to ascertain what happened in Spain; the defendant is never asked to testify about the facts of the case; no witnesses are called. Instead, the judges review the relative merits of the pleas, then hear the formal accusation of Charles and the equally formal denial of Ganelon.

There is no disagreement whatever about the facts: Ganelon freely admits he plotted the deaths of Roland and the entire rear guard in league with the pagans Blancandrin and Marsilla. The question before the court is one of law rather than of equity, namely: did Ganelon's action constitute treason? The king says it did; Ganelon says no, and presents two lines of defense. First, he says he was justified in seeking to avenge himself on his stepson: Roland had committed certain unspecified wrongs against him in the past, depriving him of wealth and possessions, and furthermore had insulted him by nominating him for the embassy to Marsilla. Second, Ganelon reminds the court that he had made a public *defi*, or challenge, to Roland, Olivier, and the Twelve Peers of France in the presence of Charles and his great lords, which automatically clears him of any charge of subterfuge, a *sine qua non* of the crime of treason. In summary, Ganelon claims that his act was one of openly declared, justified vengeance, not treason against his lord and country.

Following each stage of the proceedings, the members of the court withdraw to deliberate the arguments they have heard. According to proper judicial procedure, once all the pleas have been presented and considered, a verdict should be forthcoming, based solely on the merits of the case. But at this point in the trial medieval justice miscarries: because of precisely the same kind of irresolution that caused the Franks in Charlemagne's army to leap at the chance for a truce with Marsilla, the judges, swayed by the men from Auvergne, put expediency and personal safety before principle. Prompted by fear of Pinabel's wrath, they call upon Charles to abandon his suit and let Ganelon go unpunished. The king is understandably infuriated by this display of spinelessness, which leaves both himself and his empire unavenged, and hence disgraced. Yet, since he has given the *seniores* jurisdiction in the case, he is powerless to act in his own behalf.

At this critical moment, a new voice is heard; Count Thierry steps forward to defend the cause of Charles. Acting as a self-appointed judge, he delivers a minority verdict denouncing that given by the court. Thierry argues that Roland, by virtue of the command given him, was an official deputy of the king and should have enjoyed immunity from personal attacks for the duration of his service; therefore, his betrayal by Ganelon amounted to betrayal of Charles himself, and was an act of treason. His verdict is immediately contested by Pinabel; representing both his family and the opinion of the court, he presents a formal rebuttal by calling Thierry a liar.

Suddenly the proceedings have shifted to an entirely different plane. In effect, a new trial has begun, a *judicium dei*, or trial before God, the outcome of which will be determined by the principles of the success theory. The question now, both a legal and moral one, is simply this:

who is right, Pinabel or Thierry? The issue will be decided by judicial combat, during which it is assumed that God will intervene personally and uphold the contestant who is right, so that justice may prevail. Because of the gravity of the accusations, this will be a fight to the death; if the defeated man is not killed on the field, he will be hanged afterwards.

Preparations for the battle are carried out with a scrupulous concern for protocol:

1. Both men temporarily hand over their fiefs to Charles, since the holdings of the loser will revert to him.

2. Pinabel offers thirty hostages to vouch for his appearance and proper conduct at the battle, while Charles pledges himself as surety for Thierry.

3. The court sets the time and place of the battle.

4. Servants bring in benches for the combatants and their followers to sit on while the referee, a distinguished nobleman selected by the court to act as *porte-parole*, carries back and forth the prescribed declarations of innocence, reads aloud the charges, and explains the rules which will govern the battle.

5. The combatants fulfill their religious obligations by attending a special mass for their souls, making generous contributions to their churches, and confessing.

6. They retire briefly to arm themselves, and return ready for battle.

In the combat that follows, the author takes some pains to stress Pinabel's physical superiority to his opponent, even going so far as to say, "when he hits someone his time is up" (v. 3840). But though Thierry is hit, his time is decidedly *not* up; he weathers the best Pinabel can offer, is miraculously spared from death, and goes on to win. Divine intervention has proved him, and by extension Charles, to be in the right, and in accordance with God's verdict the court sentences Ganelon to a traitor's death.

Here, by medieval custom, the matter should have ended. What baffles students of the *Song of Roland* is the strange decision of the court to execute Pinabel's thirty kinsmen. These men had only warranted that their champion would appear at the prescribed time and place and obey the rules of the battle; when he fulfilled these conditions, they expected to be released. But it would seem that the norm does not apply here, that once again expediency governs the course of Frankish policy, and that the mass execution was occasioned more by fear of retribution than by the imperatives of heavenly or mundane justice. At any rate, this final act of the court does not follow the dictates of medieval justice, and would have been considered harsh and brutal even in the Age of Iron.

A story of men at war, the *Song of Roland* was designed to appeal to a predominantly military audience, and many details of equipage and weaponry taken for granted by the poet now need to be explained. Einhard describes Charlemagne's apparel in this way:

> He wore his national—that is, Frankish—dress. He was attired in shirt and underwear of linen, followed by a tunic with a silk fringe and leggings; then his legs were cross-gartered and his feet put into shoes; and in winter he protected his shoulders and chest with a jacket made from the skins of otters or ermine. He wore a blue cloak and always carried a sword with a hilt and belt of either gold or silver. Occasionally he used a jeweled sword, but only at important festivals or when envoys came from foreign nations.[9]

When dressing for battle, the medieval knight added to his everyday clothing a gambeson, a hauberk or byrnie, and a helmet. The gambeson, which was worn over the characteristic Frankish tunic, was a thick jacket quilted with either wool batting or shredded rags. The oldest and most widespread type of body armor known, it was used by ancient Egyptian troops, and is even today the Chinese soldier's first line of defense. Although it offers little protection against a thrusting weapon such as the lance, it is quite effective in warding off sword-cuts and arrows fired from a distance. European infantrymen of the Middle Ages normally wore gambesons as their sole defense, while cavalrymen used them beneath their outer armor to cushion the shock of blows.

The knight's principal defensive garment was either a byrnie or a hauberk. The vestlike byrnie was generally made of a material called *cuir-bouilli,* which was leather boiled in oil until it was soft and then molded to fit the torso; when dry it was very tough and resistant to cutting blows. The hauberk was a knee-length cloth tunic made with slits front and rear, like a riding skirt, and often equipped with an integral coif which had a small opening in it for the face. This garment was reinforced by any of several kinds of metallic armor. The most common variety, called *scale* or *imbricate,* consisted of small plates sewn to the fabric beneath in overlapping rows. Though it was quite serviceable and permitted easy movement, scale armor had one serious drawback: it was immensely heavy. The weight problem was finally solved by the introduction of the more costly chain mail, with its fine mesh of interlocking wire rings. Of Oriental origin, chain mail was first known and imitated in Europe by the Romans, who saw it on Scythian and Parthian cavalrymen, but the time and expense required to make it kept it from being very widely used except by the most affluent.

The conical Norman helmet, or *casque,* was made of four triangular metal plates riveted together in a ring and converging at their apexes. Frequently it was furnished with a *nasal,* a narrow metal flange attached to the front of the helmet and projecting downward in front of the nose, and designed not to stop a right-angle blow but only to deflect the descending path of a sword and thus protect the face.

Evidence of eighth- and ninth-century styles in military apparel suggests that the defensive armor of Charlemagne's time was somewhat less elaborate than that described in the *Song of Roland.* The Frankish hauberk, for instance, was probably just a simple jacket reinforced by *pourpointerie,* metal rings sewn on at spaced intervals, and the casque little more than a plain leather cap. In the relief adorning the church lintel at Angoulême, Christian and pagan cavalrymen are seen engaged in battle, and barring a few minor details such as the shape of the shield and the Christians' fondness for long veils flowing down from beneath their helmets, all the combatants dress very much alike.

The primary offensive weapon of the medieval knight was the lance. Descended from the Oriental javelin and originally intended to be thrown, the lance had evolved during the Middle Ages into an exclusively aristocratic thrusting weapon. Its sturdy wooden shaft, commonly of ash, was attached to the head by means of a hollowed-out iron socket about eighteen inches in length. Forged in one piece with the socket, the lancehead was usually leaf- or lozenge-shaped, and was invariably provided with a narrow strip of cloth which served the same purpose as the blood-groove of a sword or bayonet, preventing the head from becoming inextricably lodged in the body of an opponent. In time this little pennant outgrew its utilitarian origin and became the most prized ornament of the medieval knight. As the art of heraldry slowly developed, it became the immediate ancestor of the armorial banners and ensigns which were proudly flown everywhere as guidons and identifying symbols. When an army was on the march, these pennants were kept neatly furled upon the lance shafts—*fermées* is the technical term—but at the first sign of battle they were unrolled and flown with a brave show of color to lift morale and dismay the enemy. They were just as useful in bivouac as in battle; knights planted their lances outside their tents with pennants unfurled as a handy means of recognition, and by analogy flew them from the walls of conquered cities to betoken victory.

Only when a knight was unhorsed or in some way deprived of the use of his lance did he turn to his secondary weapon, the sword. The characteristic Frankish sword, forged from a single steel billet, was about thirty inches long and had a broad, double-edged blade which ran with very little taper to a rather obtuse point. It had short, simple quillons or cross-guards, a straight grip, and a flaring or slightly bulbous pommel. It rode in a metal-lined leather scabbard which was often covered in linen and then painted and hardened with wax to a brilliant luster. The scabbard was hung about the waist by a small cord and worn on the left hip underneath the hauberk. In order that the sword might be quickly accessible, the hauberk was provided with a slit through which the hilt protruded.

Although it ranked second to the lance on the battlefield, the sword always enjoyed a ritual eminence far beyond its actual value as a weapon. Possibly through Oriental influence, ceremonial swords were elaborately damascened and their blades engraved with mottoes and magical symbols and signs of the zodiac. Furthermore, the sword played a significant role in feudal society: knighthood could be conferred only with the sword; together with the scepter and the orb, it was the third major insignia of imperial power; and in solemn processions it was always carried before the sovereign, its blade pointed skyward as a sign of triumphant military power and justice.

Nor was the sword associated only with earthly sovereignty; sanctified by the Church at the time of the Crusades, it became the universal symbol of the union of spiritual and mundane militancy. Of course, ever since the days of Achilles' shield, fine weapons have possessed an irresistible appeal for the men who use them. Roland's Durendal and Olivier's Halteclere and Charles's *Joyeuse* are treated with the same special faith and almost superstitious affection any soldier feels for the tools that keep him alive and victorious in battle. The ancient Scandinavian heroes also gave names to their swords, and in Russia as late as the nineteenth century magic spells were still being spoken over swords to enhance their efficacy in battle. But as a Christian symbol the sword acquired even more than ordinary significance. Its shape made it inevitably a makeshift crucifix in times of exigency on the battlefield, and it frequently was used in the last rites of men killed in action. It is therefore not surprising that Durendal should have within its pommel priceless religious relics, or that Roland in his dying speech should address it as the emblem of military and divine power.

A final weapon carried by the Frankish man-at-arms, a large knife which looked much like a scaled-down replica of the sword, was probably used much more in hunting and everyday camp life than in combat. Weapons other than these, especially throwing weapons, were scorned by the Christian nobility, and throughout the *Song of Roland* are seen only in the hands of the pagans. Although the early Franks were reputed to favor a heavy, double-bitted throwing ax, by the time of the Crusades such weapons were associated with heathens and the commonalty. The contempt for javelins and bows in particular was a social one, since these had long been infantry weapons; in fact, the feeling against them was so intense that in 1139 the Roman

Catholic Church officially banned the use of arrows against Christians.

Unlike most of the implements of warfare, which changed very little in the years between Roncesvals and Hastings, the Frankish shield did show considerable variation. In the ninth century it was modeled closely on the Roman buckler, a small, round metal shield made with a projecting boss or *umbo* in its center. This style predominated in Europe through the tenth century, and was still common well into the eleventh, when it was gradually supplanted by a new model, Oriental in origin, but known in the West long before the Crusades: the tall, almond-shaped shield, constructed of leather or *cuir-bouilli* stretched over a wooden frame, and slung from the neck by a strap called a *guige*. On its padded inner side two leather loops were provided for the left arm and hand to pass through, so that a knight could keep hold of his horse's reins while still protecting his body. Since Homer's time the shield had offered the artist an ideal surface to demonstrate his skill upon, and the shields of all the warriors in the *Song of Roland,* both Moslem and Christian, are to be visualized as gaily painted with geometrical designs and fabulous birds and beasts.

The most important item of a knight's equipment was, of course, his horse. Actually, three different kinds of horses were taken along on a military campaign: the pack-horse or *sumter;* a smooth-gaited riding horse called the *palfrey;* and a fast, big-boned war horse or *destrier,* so called because he was normally led on the right side of the palfrey. In the early Middle Ages elaborate metal armor had not as yet been developed for horses, and their only protection consisted of a heavy quilted cloth designed to fend off arrows and oblique sword-cuts.

III

Sir Kenelm Digby (1603–65), soldier, diplomat, traveler, and amateur philosopher and scientist, was also a great collector of old manuscripts, which he loved to assemble and mark with his coat of arms. A number of years before his death he donated well over two hundred ancient manuscripts to Oxford University, among which was a peculiar little parchment containing two texts dating from the early Middle Ages and written in different hands: a copy of the Chalcidius translation of Plato's *Timaeus* and the now-famous Oxford version of the *Song of Roland*. The manuscript has a small format and is written in a script paleographers call "Roman miniscule," which was quite common in the early part of the twelfth century.

The Oxford manuscript is without question the work of a scribe rather than the author, and a rather careless scribe at that. But strangely enough, it is his very laxity and inattentiveness which marks this text as a particularly good one. To resolve this paradox, one must know something about the nature of medieval manuscripts. Practically all the writings which have come down to us from the Middle Ages are what scholars call "composites," and represent the combined efforts of the author and every scribe who got his hands on the work. Respect for the inviolability of a literary text is a quite recent attitude, and scribes, considering themselves editors and collaborators as well as amanuenses, seldom hesitated to rework and "improve" a piece of writing in the process of copying it down. The upshot of all this is a vast divergence among the extant copies of virtually all medieval works, with each copy showing its own characteristic patchwork of variants and errors. In general, a medieval text bears comparison not with a carefully edited modern edition done from the author's manuscript and checked for accuracy at every stage of its production but with a set of notes taken from a pirated reprint of an amateurishly hand-set edition done by a small-town job printer with a drinking problem. Thus, from the scholar's point of view, a "good" text is not necessarily a flawless one, but simply one that shows little or no deliberate scribal tampering and indicates by the nature of its mistakes that the scribe was content to copy his source in a perfunctory fashion.

The Oxford version, all scholars agree, is the best and oldest extant text of the *Song of Roland*: 3998 lines of verse divided into 291 paragraphs, and written in the Anglo-Norman French of the early twelfth century. But it is by no means the only text; no less than six other Old French versions of the poem have been discovered, all

of them markedly inferior to the Oxford, but each interesting in its own right to students of the *chanson de geste*.
They are:

V⁴: Number IV of the French Collection in the Library
of San Marco, in Venice. Written in a strange literary
conglomerate of Italian and French, it consists of 6012
lines divided into 413 paragraphs, and dates from the
fourteenth century.

V⁷: Number VII from the same collection. It has 8880
lines in rhymed strophes, and apparently was copied in
Italy around the close of the thirteenth century.

C: The Chateauroux manuscript, another long rhymed
version much like V⁷, and originally part of the collection
of Louis XVI at Versailles.

P: The Paris text, consisting of 373 rhymed strophes in
a Germanic French dialect, and dating from the thirteenth
century.

L: Manuscript Number 984 of the public library at
Lyons, France, a fragmentary version of the Roland story
grafted onto an Arthurian tale, consisting of 2933 lines in
rhymed strophes.

T: A manuscript from the west of France now held by
Trinity College, Cambridge, which consists of 5705 lines
in rhymed strophes and was written around the end of the
fifteenth century.

One step further from the original stand a number of
rather free translations of the *Song of Roland*. The best-
known of these are the *Ruolandsliet* by the Bavarian priest
Konrad, which dates from the latter half of the twelfth
century; and Part VIII of the Old Norse *Karlamagnussaga,*
a collection of stories about Charlemagne assembled by
Robert the Monk at the behest of the Norwegian king
Haakon Haakonsson, a great fan of the *chansons de geste*.

After examining in detail the relative merits of all these
works, most scholars have accepted the following hypoth-
eses: (1) All the versions of the poem we have today
descend ultimately from a common ancestor, an early text
which is lost; (2) the Oxford manuscript is a first revision of this lost text, while all the other Old French
versions derive from another, missing first revision; therefore, (3) any line from the Oxford text carries exactly the
same weight as all the other versions put together.

For these reasons modern editors concede the *précellence* of the Oxford manuscript and tamper with it as little as possible, using the other versions only when absolutely necessary to amend glaring scribal errors and omissions. In accordance with this practice, the translation presented here follows the conservative edition of Joseph Bédier, garnished sparingly with variant readings suggested by more recent scholarship.

Once in a while a man comes along who seems to have been born more for literature than for the world he inhabits, whose very being seems overshadowed by the archetype it embodies. Such a man was Count Roland. In Einhard's biography an historical personage of moderate significance identified merely as "the prefect of the Breton frontier," he was only one among several more important men killed at Roncesvals. But even in the annals of history this view becomes clouded by conflicting evidence: two small gold coins dating from the time of Charlemagne have been discovered which bear on one side the legend *Car/lus* and on the other *Rod/lan,* and immediately a suspicion arises that Roland may have been a more illustrious man than Einhard will allow, even that the mysterious rumor of the "secret sin" of Charlemagne which kept cropping up throughout the Middle Ages, cannot be peremptorily ignored. When we add to all this the strangeness of his name, which may come from *hroþi*, the Germanic word for "fame" and which was apparently unknown in France before his time, already the hard, bright details of history begin to dissolve into the twilight of myth and legend.

Then, after more than three hundred years of silence, the Roland of the poem steps into view: dauntless chevalier cut from the same cloth as the great crusader heroes Bohemond and Tancred and Baldwin; fervently pious defender of the faith like Baudry of Dol and St. Hugh of Cluny; martyr in the grand style of St. Sebastian; faithful friend to his companions Olivier and Turpin; and loyal vassal to his liege lord Charles. In all his actions Roland is the medieval nobleman *par excellence*—he rides to war as he rides to the hunt, with casual abandon; he captures towns and vast amounts of plunder simply for the pleasure

of turning them over to his king; his idea of a good joke is
to bring Charles an "orb" in the form of apple. After a day
of hunting or fighting he enjoys nothing better than to
spend the evening reveling in his lord's great hall, where,
along with the other men in Charlemagne's *maisnee*, he
makes the customary boasts, desiring above all else that
his name may never be sullied by satirical songs.

Seen in relation to the crusading spirit of the eleventh
century, Roland's behavior is in no way unusual. Modern
critics who choose to regard him as a blood-thirsty fanatic
defiling the pacifist principles of early Christianity commit
the blunder of wresting Roland from the world he in-
habited. To substitute the prejudices of one's own era for
those of another may be an amusing parlor game for the
amateur ethicist, but it has no place in a serious study of
literature. To twelfth-century France, Roland died the
glorious death of a Christian martyr. Throughout the
poem he is depicted as a tireless servant to the causes of
both his feudal and his spiritual lords. Though the other
Franks, even the emperor himself, let personal interests
cloud their better judgment, Roland never wavers in his
resolve to hold out for total victory. Of all the Christians
in Spain, he alone realizes what it will take the object-
lesson of a Roncesvals to demonstrate—that there can be
no compromise with paganism. Later on, when he stead-
fastly refuses Olivier's entreaties to call for reinforcements,
Roland is still the same man he always was. He recognizes
that Olivier's way—the "practical" way—can at best lead
to another *détente* with Marsilla and consequently only
prolong the issue, whereas a gesture of bold sacrifice will
force the Franks to make a dedicated commitment against
the Saracens—in other words, a crusade.

Seen in the broadest sense, Roland's folly transcends
the everyday wisdom and prudence of Olivier. The common sense and prudence of the Franks have only served
to lead the rear guard into an ambush; what is needed now
is an audacious move that will elicit an all-out effort from
Charles. It is interesting to observe that the lesser characters of the poem, like many critics, invariably fail to
comprehend this reasoning: Olivier regards the loss of the
rear guard as a senseless waste, and Ganelon confidently
assures Marsilla that Charles will lose his taste for war

once Roland is dead. Neither of them understands that psychologically the emperor is just like Roland, and will react exactly as Roland has anticipated he must. Turpin, by the way, the third person of this militant medieval trinity, seems to intuit Roland's purpose when he predicts in detail the effect the massacre will have on Charlemagne and the main body of Franks.

Those who side with Olivier and the temporizing Franks often box themselves in with specious reasoning of this sort: (1) Roland is a hero who comes to grief; hence, he must be a tragic hero, and the poem must be a tragedy. (2) The downfall of a tragic hero must be occasioned by a flaw in his character (usually *desmesure*, "lack of moderation," is instanced here). (3) Since the poem is a tragedy dealing with the suffering brought on by Roland's flawed character, the long Baligant episode violates the unity of action and needlessly delays the ending.

But the simple facts remain that the poem is *not* a tragedy, and Roland is *not* a tragic hero, but a martyr. Martyrs do not have tragic flaws; unlike ordinary men they participate in a higher reality, beyond the requisites of human reason and common sense. In a metaphysical sense, every martyr is a *Christomimetes*, an impersonator of Christ, who becomes through his act of self-sacrifice a brief but genuine reincarnation of Christ on earth. Though Olivier, like Vergil in the *Divine Comedy*, represents the best a man can hope for without the aid of divine grace, Roland, like Christ, can transform the humiliation of earthly defeat into spiritual victory. The resounding triumph of Christianity over paganism in the climactic duel of Charles and Baligant is made possible only through the martyrdom of Roland, and the loss of the rear guard is thus vindicated by the greater victory.

For a brief look at Charlemagne, we may turn once more to his contemporary biographer. In a formal portrait Einhard describes him this way:

He was large and robust of body, tall in stature but not disproportionately so, for his height was seven times the length of his foot. The top of his head was round, his eyes extremely large and darting, his nose a bit larger than average, his hair beautiful and white, and his ex-

pression gay and cheerful, so that he appeared dignified
and imposing when seated as well as when standing.
Although his neck was rather thick and short and his
stomach seemed to protrude, these things were not notice-
able because of the good proportions of the rest of his
body. His walk was steady and his entire carriage manly;
his voice was clear, though less powerful than the size
of his body might lead one to expect.[10]

This was the historical Charles. Commander in chief of
the Franks, third in the line of great Carolingian allies of
the Church, empire builder and crusader, notorious liber-
tine, and semibarbaric feudal lord in the old Germanic
tradition, he was only thirty-six years of age at the time
of the Spanish campaign and would not be an emperor
until 800, nor called "magnus" until 801. However, even
during his lifetime Charles was on his way to becoming in
the popular imagination the godlike patriarch we see in the
poem. He acquired a borrowed splendor from the past by
reviving in the minds of his subjects almost forgotten
memories of ancient Rome. He initiated a brief classical
renascence at his court in Aix; he had his name engraved
on Roman coins; he led numerous campaigns against the
enemies of the Church; and—most important of all—by
assuming the title of Holy Roman Emperor, he gave hope
to all men who dreamed of a New Jerusalem and a stable
world order. All these actions stirred up visions of the
ancient caesars and the *pax romana.* One of his court
scholars, an Irishman by the name of Dungal, even went
so far as to bolster the resemblance by manufacturing a
glorious classical ancestry for the Franks, proclaiming that
they, like the Romans of the *Aeneid,* were direct descend-
ants of the Trojans.

By the time of the *Song of Roland,* Charles had passed
over completely into legend. He is now the Ancient of
Days, the colossal figure whose mighty presence encom-
passes the poem from first to last. The leader of all Christendom in an endless crusade against the inroads of the
pagans, he is the executive arm of the Church and the
favorite of God, Who has given him twelve noble peers
as He gave His Son twelve apostles, and Who regularly
sends him instructions through dreams. He wages war not

for plunder or pleasure or glory, but solely to expand the frontiers of the Christian world and to save the souls of the unbaptized heathen. He is incredibly old—almost two hundred, some say—and has fought on every front against the pagans, yet he still has the strength and vigor to defeat the mighty emir in single combat. The years have weakened him, as they weaken all men—they make him particularly susceptible to Marsilla's tempting offer of a truce —but at the same time, they endue him with vast authority over his Franks and give him the unrelenting will to avenge the death of his nephew, come what may.

The character of Archbishop Turpin offers a strong case for the influence of the First Crusade on the *Song of Roland*. Everything about this fire-eating clergyman suggests that his brand of Christianity is precisely that endorsed by Urban II at Clermont. The historical Turpin, archbishop of Reims from 753 to 794 and obviously not among those present at Roncesvals, is only a name in the chronicles, while the Turpin of the poem, who guarantees martyrdom to the men in the rear guard and single-handedly kills over four hundred Saracens and makes fun of cloistered monks, is of a piece with the famous fighting bishop Adhemar of Le Puy, who led a division of crusaders at the siege of Antioch. Though it was customary in medieval Europe for members of the clergy to accompany military expeditions to bless the troops before battle, assist the dying and wounded, and administer last rites, Turpin goes far beyond what would have been expected of him. Unlike many clerics he does not consider himself a noncombatant, nor does he fear the Biblical injunction, "They that take the sword shall perish with the sword," which caused some literal-minded churchmen to favor variations of the battle mace euphemistically called "morning stars" and "holy-water sprinklers." Turpin carries the same weapons as the knights in the field, and his single combats, directed with great gusto against the most heretical pagans, are described exactly like those of Roland and Olivier and the other Franks.

A count of France, brother-in-law of Charles, stepfather of Roland, and traitor to them all, Ganelon appears, quite understandably, to have no historical counterpart. His origin probably lies in the stock character of myth and folklore, the Mean Old Man. Before the action of the poem begins, he has already won a reputation for greed, and his resentment toward Roland seems to have its source in his envy of Roland's wealth and self-confidence. Later on this rancor is further deepened when Roland insults him publicly, by recommending him for the embassy to King Marsilla. It is not that Ganelon fears for his life— once in Saragossa he conducts himself with fierce audacity —but he is enraged that his stepson should suggest his name just after the emperor has specifically ruled out Naimes, Roland, Olivier, Turpin, and the other peers. Though Roland may naïvely imagine he is conferring a signal honor on his stepfather, Ganelon, already resentful and envious, sees in his act an implication that he is expendable.

These are the immediate, personal motives for Ganelon's betrayal. In the broader framework of the poem's allegory, however, where the struggle between Christianity and paganism is taking place, Ganelon's rôle is to illustrate the disastrous consequences to oneself and others brought on by an excessive love of earthly goods and pleasures. In this he differs little from most of his countrymen; through weariness, personal suffering, and disaffection for what seems to them an endless war, practically all the Franks have forgotten that the issues at stake in Spain cannot be settled with hostages and promises. It is because of this conciliatory attitude, rather than any diabolical scheme concocted between Ganelon and Marsilla, that Roland will die, Thierry will be forced to put his life on the line and, ironically, Ganelon will "renounce all he has defended in order to confront all he fears."[11]

The opening paragraph of the *Song of Roland* will serve well to illustrate the form of the entire poem:

> Carles li reis,   nostre emperere magnes,
> Set anz tuz pleins   ad estet en Espaigne:
> Tresqu'en la mer   cunquist la tere altaigne.
> N'i ad castel   ki devant lui remaigne;
> Mur ne citet   n'i est remés a fraindre,
> Fors Sarraguce,   ki est en une muntaigne.
> Li reis Marsilie   la tient, ki Deu nen aimet.

Mahumet sert   e Apollin recleimet:
Nes poet guarder   que mals ne l'i ateignet.   AOI.

Each verse paragraph (technically it is known as a *laisse*) is formally unified by several poetic devices. Every line has ten syllables, divided roughly in the middle by a pause called a *caesura* (indicated in the specimen above by a wide space in the text), and receives a rhythmic cadence from strong stresses which fall on the fourth and tenth syllables. In addition, the lines of a *laisse* are linked to one another by the repetition at the end of each line of the same vowel sound, which is never repeated from one *laisse* to the next.

The idea of the closed form is not restricted to the mechanics of the poem. In its meaning and rhetorical structure as well, each *laisse* constitutes a tightly knit, detached entity, dependent neither syntactically nor logically upon its neighbors. The absence of coordination and subordination, called *parataxis,* has the effect of assigning to each *laisse* a certain limited quantum of story and theme, which it then develops within its narrow confines and guides toward a conclusion dictated solely by its own terms. Therefore, even though a *laisse* may proceed without formal order through a succession of abrupt, disconnected statements, its underlying rationale will inevitably be made clear by the final verse, which reveals the organic and logical shape of the whole. In the *laisse* cited above, for example, the following assertions are made without any indication of sequence or relative importance:

1. Our emperor Charles has been in Spain for seven years.

2. He has conquered every castle and city in the country except Saragossa.

3. King Marsilla holds Saragossa.

4. Marsilla does not love God, but worships Mohammed and Apollo.

And then the final line—

5. No matter what he does, Marsilla cannot avoid disaster.

This *laisse* functions in the manner of a riddle, which may be stated this way: under the given circumstances (1–4), what must occur to bring about the conclusion

(5), and why must it occur? The answers are, of course: Charles will cause the downfall of Marsilla by taking Saragossa, and this will happen because his false gods fail him.

In this spasmodic fashion the skein of plot and theme is unwound. Of course, every *laisse* in the poem does not take the form of a riddle; however, most of them do consist of a series of facts set side by side with little concern for subordination or logical coherence, which are brought into sudden, brilliant focus by a climactic final verse. This technique permits precise detail to accumulate gradually, with no construction put on it, until the end of the *laisse*, when it releases, in a burst, its total significance.

The explanation of this unusual method of storytelling may possibly be found in the way medieval man interpreted the world around him and represented it in his art. During the classical periods of Greece and Rome, artists were content by and large to regard themselves and the products of their genius as natural objects in a natural world, happy and at home within the boundaries imposed upon all things by time and space. Rather than protesting against the limitations of the human condition, the classical artist rejoices in the opportunities they give him to transform a meaningless universe into the meaningful order of art. The invisible presence of the gods and their power over man, though acknowledged, are not stressed—it is man's power to act creatively and heroically in this life that matters. All men must die, it is true, but that is merely an unpleasant stipulation in the contract which granted man life, and the last thing any intelligent man should desire is to abrogate that contract before its normal term expires. Much more praiseworthy is the struggle man puts up affirming life; the rising tension in the *Iliad* and the *Odyssey* and the *Aeneid* culminates in heroic endeavor, not martyrdom.

By the Dark Ages, however, the accepted view of reality had made an about-face. The artist of the early Middle Ages, shrinking from the visible universe and seeking union with the eternal, found himself drawn inexorably away from the natural things which live in time and occupy space, and into a stylized universe of abstraction. The emergence of nonrepresentational art always signals a retreat from the visible world, and Romanesque art was no exception; by substituting the self-sufficient, spatially enclosed forms of geometry for the flowing line which leads the eye freely through space and time, the artist replaces natural boundaries with the cult of symmetry and balance. This is not to say that medieval artists denied the created world any more than they denied the carnal nature of Christ, but only that they considered its reality to be of a secondary order of importance, significant chiefly in that it makes the ultimate, transcendent reality of the Logos accessible to mankind. This world-view regards the objects and events of everyday existence as mere symbols; all that had appeared to the classical mind as an unbroken chain of cause and effect is here seen to be a sequence of shadow-pictures projected on our senses for the purpose of giving us some advance knowledge of the "real" reality beyond. The error of the ancient world was to assume that the process of cause and effect compelled events to occur in an inevitable order. Once the element of time is removed from the equation, however, the influence of one event upon its neighbor disappears, and we are left with authentic meaning—the meaning of each discrete image in the context of the transcendent reality it figures forth. It is this view that Dante reflects when he says: "The Scripture condescends to your faculties, and attributes hand and foot to God, meaning something else."[12]

None of this should be taken to mean that the author of the *Song of Roland* was wholly engulfed by the prevailing thought of his time, or that he was ignorant of the Latin epic and its vision of reality. On the contrary, his use of dream sequences, the cataloguing of battalions, and occasional rhetorical echoes of Vergil offer sufficient proof that he was aware of his genre's illustrious past. Nevertheless, the resemblances are only incidental and superficial: as we read through the poem we are constantly reminded that classical standards of form simply do not apply here. The same paratactic structure observed with the *laisse* repeats itself at every level of composition. Each *laisse* makes a fresh start, covers a small amount of narrative ground, and then leaves off as abruptly as it began; and even the largest blocks of action follow a similar pattern. In the classical epic we are accustomed to a smooth wave of causal action which builds slowly to a crest of intensity near the end, then breaks, dissipates its energy, and ebbs to a brief conclusion. Though the time scheme may be dislocated somewhat—after all, the beginning *in medias res* and the flashback are both venerable epic devices—events are nonetheless anchored firmly in time and space. Homer seldom expands his story or retards its movement by stylistic means; rather, he manipulates the flow of time by thickening description, adding incidents, or moving into a character's memory. Similarly, Vergil is inclined to arrange events in time like beads on a string, pausing only now and then to linger over a tale from the past or the luxuriant detail of a formal simile. On the other hand, the author of the *Song of Roland,* while ostensibly never leaving the literary present and making use of the epic simile only once (vv. 1874–75), conceives of his material as a sequence of isolated moments wrenched out of the stream of time and exhibited in heavily bordered, static scenes. The early critics who challenged the authenticity of the Baligant episode because it did not follow the prescriptions of Aristotelian tragedy failed to see that the poem was never intended as a single, uninterrupted narration, but a balanced grouping of geometrical figures. The poet did not lay out a line of rising action which culminates in the death of the hero; rather, he built his poem out of four large tableaux, arranged as two matching pairs and divided in the middle. In the beginning there is the crime of Ganelon, counterpoised at the end by his punishment; and in the center the martyrdom of Roland, paired with the vengeance of Charles. The carefully balanced structure of the *Song of Roland* is designed like a folding mirror to reflect the battle between Good and Evil at all levels of meaning. Those who contend that the Baligant episode is fraudulent often cite the fact that the foreshadowing of events ends suddenly after the death of Roland, but this evidence demonstrates equally well the bilateral symmetry of the poem, dominated by the impending disaster of the Franks in the first half and their triumph in the second.

An apparent exception to paratactic structure arises in the so-called *laisses similaires,* those paragraphs which through slightly varied repetition of words and phrases seem to indicate the poet was trying to achieve some broader degree of thematic unity in time.[13] It is true that the *laisses similaires,* which have no known counterpart in earlier literature, operate thematically in the poem. Like a set of musical variations, they weave their way back and forth through a central image, momentarily suspending the progress of the narrative. Their effect, however, is neither to enrich nor comment on the story, but to release it entirely from the bonds of time, to bring the action to a momentary standstill, so that the audience may have ample leisure to contemplate its true significance. Thematic repetition of a similar variety also occurs in the ballad, but with a different end in view: in the ballad it constantly marks off successive stages of the action and reminds the audience of what has happened since that moment in the past to which the repetition refers. In the *laisse similaire,* however, each repeated line doubles back through time and returns the reader to the very same timeless instant, with the effect that this moment is expanded into a sort of eternal present which is independent of sequence or cause and effect—in other words, a paratactic reality.

To observe this phenomenon in action, think back over a set of *laisses similaires* immediately after you have read them. Try to recall exactly how a theme was first stated, and what variations it was subjected to from one *laisse* to the next, *without thinking of its immediate context in any particular laisse*. That is, see if you can isolate a thematic element from the influence of time and temporarily set your consciousness free from linear reality. The experience, if it comes, will come as a sudden flash of recognition; if it requires laborious reconstruction nothing will have been gained, for any conscious effort of the memory will only draw it back into the stream of time. Even at best, the mind cannot remain here, but will move on readily to linear context and rejoin the thread of narrative.

In summary, the poem is neither loose and episodic like the saga nor logically periodic like the classical epic, but formal and rigidly stylized as the stone figures of Roland and Olivier upon the façade of the cathedral at Chartres. One modern scholar, Eric Auerbach, has pointed out that this sort of structure is not entirely unknown in earlier literatures; something much like it may be found in the less elevated classical genres of comedy and satire. But these do not aim at the high style, tone, or seriousness to which epic aspires, and therefore will not bear close comparison with the *Song of Roland*. Only one other work of ancient literature shares the same concern for transcendent reality, combined with a simple yet elevated style and a tone of high moral purpose—the Old Testament. The search for a literary source might well end here.

NOTES

1. *Vita Karoli Magni*, ¶9.
2. Pierre Le Gentil, *The Chanson de Roland* (Cambridge, Mass., 1969), pp. 35–36. Copyright © 1969 by the President and Fellows of Harvard College.
3. Actually, the question of the origin of the *Song of Roland* is only part of a broader problem having to do with the entire genre known as the *chanson de geste*. There are some eighty of these in all, most of them dating from the twelfth century and all offering endless riddles to students of the epic-making process.
4. One of the best modern critics, Charles Knudson, makes this point particularly well when he says of the historians: "They are too quick to assume that the *Song of Roland* is a piece of propaganda for some specific cause. They are too easily impressed by occasional resemblances between the poet's creations and the events of history. Such resemblances are in the nature of things, and do not warrant jumping hastily to sweeping and highly contestable conclusions. And there is one more error which it seems to me all these scholars have committed. They have not read the *Song of Roland* enough. Of course, they have scanned the text, alert to the resemblances of a name or of some motive to the name or a motive in that segment of history to which they have chosen to attach the composition of the poem. But to read the *Song of Roland* means to read it without ulterior motive,

giving oneself completely to the poet, traveling down
the sweep of events as he leads us, viewing his heroes
with his eyes." "The Problem of the *Chanson de
Roland*," *Romance Philology* IV, p. 10.

5. *Vita Karoli Magni,* ¶7.
6. Robert S. Picciotto, "Marsile's Right Hand," *Romance
   Notes* VII, p. 208.
7. The battle cry of the Franks, *Monjoy,* apparently
   comes from *Monte Gaudia,* the "joyous hill" from
   which pilgrims first caught sight of Rome; that of the
   Saracens, which scholars think may have been *Allah
   akhbar,* "Allah is great," must have sounded to the
   Christian ear like the barking of a dog (see v. 3527).
8. Charles ffoulkes, *Armour and Weapons* (Oxford,
   1909), p. 15.
9. *Vita Karoli Magni,* ¶23.
10. *Vita Karoli Magni,* ¶22.
11. Le Gentil, p. 87.
12. *Paradiso* IV, 43–45.
13. Compare verses 62–88, 563–95, 617–33, 1017–38,
    1049–81, 1702–21, 1753–95, 1796–1850, 1952–77,
    2297–2354, 2355–96, 2881–2908, 2909–44, 3750–
    79.

SUGGESTIONS FOR FURTHER READING

TEXTS

Joseph Bédier, ed. *La Chanson de Roland* (Paris, 1966). Old French text with facing Modern French prose translation.

T. Atkinson Jenkins, ed. *La Chanson de Roland* (Boston, 1924). Old French text with detailed introduction, footnotes, and English glossary in the back.

CRITICISM

Pierre Le Gentil, *The Chanson de Roland,* tr. Frances F. Beer (Cambridge, Mass., 1969). The best general study of the poem available.

Fern Farnham, "Romanesque Design in the *Chanson de Roland,*" *Romance Philology* XVIII, pp. 143–64. An interesting essay which fits the poem into the context of medieval art.

Charles A. Knudson, "The Problem of the *Chanson de Roland,*" *Romance Philology* IV, pp. 1–15. A sensible commentary on the scholarly questions raised by the poem.

THE SONG OF ROLAND

« 1 »

Charles the king, our mighty emperor,
has been in Spain for all of seven years,
has won that haughty land down to the sea.
There is no castle still opposing him,
nor town or wall remaining to be crushed,
except the mountain city, Saragossa.
Marsilla holds it; he does not love God,
but serves Mohammed and invokes Apollo.
No matter what he does, his ruin will come. AOI

« 2 »

The king Marsilla was in Saragossa.
He went into the shadows of an orchard,
sat down upon a terrace of blue marble
with more than twenty thousand men about him.
He now addresses all his dukes and counts:
"Just hear, my lords, what troubles weigh us down!
The emperor of sweet France, Charlemagne,

has come into this country to destroy us.
I have no army fit to give him battle,
nor have I men who might put his to rout.
20   Since you're my wise men, give me your advice,
so I may rest secure from death and shame."
No pagan has a single word in answer
save Blancandrin, from the castle of Val-Fonde.

« 3 »

Among the wisest pagans, Blancandrin
was very chivalrous and dutiful
and able in the service of his lord;
and to the king he says: "Now don't despair.
Send word to Charles the proud, the overbearing,
in all good will and faithful deference,
30   and say you'll send him bears and dogs and lions,
a thousand mewed° hawks, seven hundred camels,
four hundred mules weighed down with gold and silver,
and fifty carts to form a wagon-train,
so he may pay his mercenaries well.
He has soldiered in this country long enough;
he really should return to Aix, in France.
So say you'll follow him at Michaelmas,°
and there you will receive the Christian law,
and be his man in honor and good faith.
40   If he should ask for hostages, then send them
to gain his confidence—some ten or twenty.
We'll send the sons of our own wives to him;
though it will mean his death, I'll send my own.
Much better they should lose their heads up there
than we should lose our honor and our lands,
and let ourselves be brought to beggary." AOI

« 4 »

Says Blancandrin: "By this right hand of mine,
and by the beard that waves upon my chest,
you soon will see the Frankish host decamp.

31. *mewed:* molted, and therefore ready to hunt.
37. In the early Middle Ages, St. Michael's day was September 29.

The Frenchmen will be gone to France, their land,　　50
and when each man is where he best belongs,
then Charles will be at Aix, within his chapel,
and there he'll hold high feast on Michaelmas.
The day will come, the time allotted lapse,
and he will hear no word or news of us.
The king is arrogant, his heart is cruel,
and he will have our hostages beheaded;
but it is better they should lose their heads
than we should lose bright Spain the Beautiful
and undergo such suffering and harm."　　　60
The pagans say: "It may be he is right."

« 5 »

Marsilla brought his council to an end,
then called upon Clarin of Balaguer,°
Estamarin and Eudropin his peer,
and Priamon, Guarlan, who wears a beard,
and Machiner, his uncle named Maheu,
and Joüner, Malbien of Outremer,
and Blancandrin, to tell them his decision:
the ten most vicious he has called upon.
"My lords and barons, go to Charlemagne—　　70
he's at the siege of the town of Cordova.
You'll carry olive branches in your hands,
which signify humility and peace.
If by your skill you bring about a pact,
then I shall pay you well in gold and silver
and lands and fiefs, as much as you desire."
The pagans say: "We're quite well satisfied." AOI

« 6 »

Marsilla brought his council to an end.
He tells his men: "My lords, be on your way;
you'll carry olive branches in your hands,　　80
and say for me to Charlemagne the king

63–67. Balaguer is a town on the river Segre in Catalonia; the
other names in this passage seem to be inventions of the author.
Henceforth, only those proper names which have been reasonably
well identified will be annotated.

that for his God's sake he should pity me.
Before he sees a single month go by,
I'll follow with a thousand of my faithful,
in order to receive the Christian law
and be his man in loyalty and love.
Of course, he'll have what hostages he wants."
"You'll get a splendid pact," says Blancandrin. AOI

« 7 »

Marsilla had them bring the ten white mules
90 the king of Suatilie had sent to him;
their bits are set with gold, their saddles silver.
The men who were to take the message mounted;
they carried olive branches in their hands,
and came to Charles, who holds sway over France:
he can't entirely keep from being tricked. AOI

« 8 »

The emperor is gay and confident,
for Cordova is his; its walls are crushed,
its towers leveled by his mangonels.°
Vast plunder has been captured by his knights
100 of silver, gold, and rich accoutrements.
No pagan still remains within the town
who has not died or else become a Christian.
The emperor is in a spacious orchard,
along with Roland and Olivier,
the duke Sanson and Anseïs the Proud,
the standard-bearer Gefrey of Anjou;
Gerin and Gerier were also there,
and with them there were many other men:
no less than fifteen thousand from sweet France.
110 The chevaliers are seated on white spreads:
for entertainment, some are playing tables;°
the older and the wiser sit at chess,
and carefree bachelors practice swordsmanship.
Beneath a pine, beside an eglantine,

98. *mangonels:* military engines used for throwing stones, javelins,
etc.
111. *tables:* a dice game similar to backgammon.

there stood a throne of finest beaten gold;
here seated is the king who rules sweet France.
His beard is white, his hair is shot with gray,
his body is well formed, his features proud.
No one would need to have him pointed out.
And here the messengers got down on foot,   120
saluting him with all good will and love.

« 9 »

The first of all to speak was Blancandrin;
he tells the king: " 'May you be saved by God
the Glorious, Whom we should all adore!'
These words the valiant king Marsilla sends you;
quite deeply he has probed salvation's law,
and from his wealth would send you precious gifts
of bears and lions, greyhounds on the leash,
a thousand mewed hawks, seven hundred camels,
four hundred mules with gold and silver laden,   130
and fifty carts to form a wagon-train.
There'll be so many solid gold bezants°
that you may pay your mercenaries well.
Your sojourn in this country has been long—
you really should return to Aix, in France;
my lord will follow you, he gives his word."
The emperor lifts up his hands toward God,
then bows his head, begins to speculate. AOI

« 10 »

The emperor still held his head bowed down,
for he was never hasty in his speech;   140
by habit, he speaks only at his leisure.
And when he raises up, his face is stern.
He tells the messengers: "You've spoken well,
but King Marsilla is my greatest foe.
About these words which you have said just now—
to what extent may I put faith in them?"
"By hostages," replies the Saracen,
"of which you shall have ten, fifteen, or twenty;

132. *bezants:* Oriental coins known throughout Western Europe.

I'll send a son of mine, on pain of death,
150   and you shall have still nobler, I believe.
When, at your royal palace, you attend
the high feast of Saint Michael of the Peril,°
my lord will come to you, as he has said,
and in those baths° God fashioned for you there,
he wishes to receive the Christian faith."
Charles answers: "Even yet he may be saved." AOI

« 11 »

The evening was clear, the sunset bright:
King Charles commands the ten mules to be stabled
and has a tent pitched in the spacious orchard,
160   in which the ten envoys are billeted;
twelve sergeants have attended to them well;
they spent the night there till the break of day.
The emperor has risen in the morning;
the king has heard his matins and his mass,
and then the king has gone beneath a pine
and called his barons to conclude his council:
he always wants the Frenchmen to advise him. AOI

« 12 »

The emperor goes underneath a pine
and calls his barons up to give him counsel:
170   Archbishop Turpin and the duke Oger,°
Richard the Old° and his descendant Henry,°
from Gascony the bold count Acelin,
Milon, Thibaud of Reims, his cousin;
Gerin and Gerier were also there—
together with the others came Count Roland

152. This famous monastery on the coast of France was known as *Sanctus Michael in periculo maris* because of the treacherous tidal flats between it and the mainland.
154. Charles's palace at Aix was built over artesian springs.
170–71. Oger the Dane is a literary hero in his own right—a *chanson de geste* deals with his adventures. Richard the Old is probably Richard I, duke of Normandy (d. 996), and his descendant Henry may be a complimentary reference to William the Conqueror's son.

and valorous, well-born Olivier—
more than a thousand Franks from France were there.
And Ganelon the traitor came there, too.
The council that gave rise to grief now starts. AOI

« 13 »

"My lords and barons," says the emperor,   *180*
"the king Marsilla sent me messengers:
he wants to give me vast gifts from his wealth—
bears and lions, greyhounds on the leash,
a thousand mewed hawks, seven hundred camels,
four hundred mule-loads of Arabian gold,
along with more than fifty heavy carts—
and further says, if I go back to France,
he'll follow me to Aix, and in my palace,
he swears he will receive our holy law,
become a Christian, hold his lands from me—   *190*
but still I'm not quite sure of his intent."
The Frenchmen say: "We'll do well to be careful!" AOI

« 14 »

The emperor has stated the proposal.
Count Roland, who does not approve of it,
stands up and starts to speak in opposition.
He tells the king: "You're wrong to trust Marsilla!
We've been in Spain for all of seven years;
I conquered for you Noples and Commibles,
I took Valterne and all the land of Pine,
and Balaguer, Tudela,° and Sezille.   *200*
There King Marsilla showed his treachery:
some fifteen of his pagans he dispatched,
each carrying with him an olive branch;
they said the very same words to you then.
You let your Franks advise you what to do—
they recommended something very foolish—
you sent two of your counts out to the pagans

200. *Tudela:* A town on the Ebro not far from Saragossa.

(Basan was one, the other one was Basil)°
who promptly took their heads near Haltilie!°
210 Keep waging war the way you started out,
lead your assembled host to Saragossa,
lay siege to it, for all your life is worth,
and take revenge on those the villains killed." AOI

« 15 »

The emperor, his head as yet bent down,
tugs gently at his beard, smoothes his moustache,
but tells his nephew neither yes nor no.
The Franks are silent—all but Ganelon;
he rises to his feet and goes to Charles,
most haughtily begins his argument,
220 and tells the king: "You're wrong to trust a lackey,
or me, or anyone, unless you gain!
When King Marsilla thus sends word to you
that with clasped hands he will become your man
and govern all of Spain by your permission,
and that he will receive the law we keep,
whoever says we should reject this plea
does not care, sire, what kind of death we die.
Vainglorious advice should not prevail.
Ignoring fools, let's cleave unto the wise!" AOI

« 16 »

230 Immediately thereafter Naimes° came forth
(the court has never had a better vassal)
and told the king: "Now you have heard it well,
just how Count Ganelon has answered you;
his words seem wise to me, if understood.
In warfare King Marsilla has been vanquished—
you've taken from him all his fortresses,
your mangonels have smashed his walls to bits,

208. The story of the ill-fated mission of Basan and Basil is known
in other medieval literary works, but is unknown historically.
209. Haltilie may be simply the Spanish *altillo* (hill).
230. Historically Duke Naimes is only a name—that of a Gascon
lord who paid homage to Charlemagne—but in medieval legend
he became famous as a wise adviser.

you've burned his cities, overwhelmed his men:
now when he pleads for you to show him mercy,
to keep on fighting him would be a sin.   240
With hostages he'll guarantee your safety,
and this great conflict need go on no more."
The Frenchmen say: "The duke has spoken well." AOI

« 17 »

"My lords and barons, whom are we to send
to Saragossa, to the king Marsilla?"
Duke Naimes replies: "I'll go there, by your leave.
Just let me have the gauntlet and the staff."
The king gives answer: "You're a brilliant man,
and by this beard and this moustache of mine,
you'll never go so far away from me;   250
so keep your seat when no one calls on you."

« 18 »

"My lords and barons, whom should we dispatch
to the Saracen that rules in Saragossa?"
Count Roland answers: "I can go quite well."
"You won't, that's sure," says Count Olivier,
"your heart is acrimonious and proud;
I fear that you would get into a squabble.
But if it please the king, I'd like to go."
The king replies: "Be quiet, both of you!
Nor you nor he will ever set foot there,   260
and by this beard that you see streaked with white,
the dozen peers are not to be appointed!"
The Franks, their voices silenced, do not speak.

« 19 »

Turpin of Reims arose then from the ranks
and tells the king: "Let all your Franks remain.
You've sojourned in this country seven years
and they've endured great suffering and pain.
Let me, sire, have the gauntlet and the staff,

and I'll go to the Spanish Saracen,
270 so I may get some inkling of his looks."
But testily the emperor replies:
"Sit down on that white carpet over there
and do not speak unless I tell you to. AOI

« 20 »

"French chevaliers," says Charles the emperor,
"pick out for me a baron from my marches°
to carry my dispatch to King Marsilla."
Says Roland, "Ganelon, my stepsire, is your man."
The French say, "He can do it very well:
if he's not sent, no wiser man will be."
280 At this Count Ganelon was furious,
and shrugging off his heavy marten furs,
he stands unmoving in his silk *bliaut*.
His eyes are gray, his features very fierce,
his chest is thick, his body well proportioned:
so handsome was he that his peers all stared.
"You utter fool, why rave?" he says to Roland.
"They know quite well that I am your stepsire—
yet you name me to go out to Marsilla.
If God should deign that I come back again,
290 then I shall stir up such a feud with you
that it will last as long as you're alive!"
Says Roland, "I hear pride and foolishness,
for everybody knows I fear no threat;
a messenger should be a man with sense,
and if the king desires, I'll take your place."

« 21 »

"You'll never go for me," says Ganelon, AOI
"you're not my vassal, nor am I your lord.
Charles orders me to carry out his mission;
I'll go to Saragossa, to Marsilla:
300 but first I'll have a little bit of fun
in order that I may assuage my wrath."
When Roland hears this, he begins to laugh. AOI

275. *marches:* borderlands under imperial jurisdiction.

« 22 »

Now Ganelon, on seeing Roland laugh,
is so outraged, almost convulsed with fury,
he very nearly loses consciousness.
He tells the count: "I've never cared for you;
you've had this unfair judgment passed on me!
Just Emperor, you see me here at hand;
I only wish to carry out your orders.

« 23 »

"I know well I must go to Saragossa: AOI   310
the man who goes out there cannot return.
Remember most of all: my wife's your sister,
by whom I have a son, there is no finer—
Baudoin, that is—he'll be a valiant man.
To him I leave my honors and my fiefs.
Take care of him—I'll see him nevermore."
Charles answers him: "You have too soft a heart.
When I command, it's up to you to go."

« 24 »

Whereon the king says: "Ganelon, come forward, AOI
in order to receive the staff and glove: 320
you heard it, you've been chosen by the Franks."
Says Ganelon: "Sire, Roland's done all this!
I'll lose no love on him throughout my life,
nor on Olivier, since he's his comrade,
nor the dozen peers, because they love him so—
I here defy them, sire, before your eyes!"
At this the king says: "You are too hot-tempered:
now go, for I have given the command."
"I'll go with no more guarantee of safety   AOI
than Basil or Basan his brother had."   330

306. Ganelon's statement here (*Jo ne vus aim nient*), which
sounds like a masterpiece of understatement, is a legal phrase
analogous to the language still used in diplomacy which describes
war as an "unfriendly act."

« 25 »

The emperor holds out his right-hand glove;
Count Ganelon, who'd rather not be there,
on reaching out to take it, lets it drop.
The Frenchmen say: "My God! what does this mean?
This embassy will bring us great misfortune."
"My lords," says Ganelon, "you'll hear the news.

« 26 »

"My lord," says Ganelon, "give me your leave;
since I must go, there's no need to delay."
The king then says: "In Jesus' name and mine!"
340   With his right hand he blesses and absolves him,
then puts the staff and letter in his care.

« 27 »

Count Ganelon returns to his encampment;
begins to make arrangements for his gear,
the finest he is able to obtain.
He fastened golden spurs upon his feet,
then hung his sword Murgleis upon his hip,
climbed up on Tachebrun, his destrier,
while Guinemer, his uncle, held his stirrup.
You there might see so many knights shed tears,
350   all saying, "Baron, you've had rotten luck!
You've served the king at court for many years;
those there acknowledge you a noble vassal;
whoever deemed that you should have to go
will not be saved or helped by Charlemagne.
Count Roland shouldn't have considered you;
you come from such a noble lineage."
They tell him afterward, "Oh sire, take us!"
but Ganelon replies: "Lord God forbid!
It's better I die alone than many knights.
360   But when you go back to sweet France, my lords,
on my behalf take greetings to my wife,
to Pinabel, my comrade and my peer,
and to my son Baudoin, whom you all know,
and help him and acknowledge him your lord."
He rides out to the road, is on his way. AOI

« 28 »

Beneath tall olive trees rides Ganelon
to join the Saracen ambassadors;
now Blancandrin falls back in line with him;
they talk to one another with great cunning.
Says Blancandrin: "A wondrous man is Charles,   *870*
who conquered Puglia,° all Calabria,°
and crossed the salt sea on his way to England,
where he exacted tribute for Saint Peter.°
What does he want with us, here in our marches?"
"Such is his nature," answered Ganelon,
"there'll never be a man to equal him." AOI

« 29 »

Says Blancandrin: "The Franks are noble men,
although some dukes and counts may do great harm
by counseling their lord in such a way
that he and others, too, are wronged and injured."   *880*
"That's true of no one," answers Ganelon,
"save Roland, who one day shall be disgraced.
While Charles sat in the shade the other morning,
his nephew came there, decked out in his byrnie—
he'd been out pillaging near Carcassonne.°
He held a bright red apple in his hand.
'Here, fair sire,' says Roland to his uncle,
'I offer you the crowns of all the kings.'
His arrogance will be the end of him,
for every single day he teases death.   *890*
If someone killed him, we might all have peace." AOI

« 30 »

Says Blancandrin: "A very hard man, Roland,
who wants to make all peoples recreant
and challenge every country in the world.
With whose help does he plan to do all this?"

371–73. Puglia and Calabria are, respectively, the heel and toe of
Italy. In fact, Charlemagne never conquered either province, nor
was he responsible for the "Romefee" (Peter's pence), a tax levied
in England.
385. *Carcassonne:* a city in the south of France.

Count Ganelon replies: "The Frankish men—
they think so much of him, they'll never fail him.
He lavishes upon them gold and silver
and destriers and mules and silks and armor;
the emperor gets everything he wants—
he'll win him lands from here to the Orient." AOI

400

« 31 »

Thus Ganelon and Blancandrin ride on
till each of them has promised to the other
that he will see to it that Roland dies.
They ride down roads and paths to Saragossa,
where, underneath a yew tree, they dismount.
A throne stood in the shadows of a pine,
swathed in a spread of Alexandrine silk.
And on it sat the king who rules all Spain,
with twenty thousand Saracens around him.
But no one there spoke up or said a word,
for they all wished to listen to the news.
Now here are Ganelon and Blancandrin.

410

« 32 »

Now Blancandrin has come before Marsilla,
his hand upon the fist of Ganelon,
and to the king he says: "Mohammed save you,
Apollo, too, whose sacred laws we keep!
We've carried out your embassy to Charles;
he lifted both his hands up toward the sky
and praised his god, but made no other answer.
He sends you here a noble lord of his—
a very wealthy° man who comes from France—
from him you'll hear if you'll have peace or not."
Marsilla says: "Now let him speak; we'll hear him."
AOI

420

« 33 »

Count Ganelon had thought out everything;
with great discretion he begins to speak

422. of *riche* generally means both "rich" and "powerful."

(as only one who really knows how can)
and to the king he says: "Be saved by God
the Glorious, whom we should all adore!
Thus noble Charlemagne requires of you   *430*
that you receive the holy Christian faith,
and he will give you half of Spain in fief.
If you will not agree to this accord,
by force you shall be taken captive, bound,
transported to the capital at Aix,
at which place you shall be condemned to death,
and there you'll die in squalor and disgrace."
At this the king Marsilla was enraged;
he seized upon a golden-headed spear
and would have thrown it, had he not been checked.   *440*
    AOI

« 34 »

The color changed in King Marsilla's face;
a tremor shook the handle of his spear.
When Ganelon sees this, he grips his sword,
unsheathing it about two fingers' breadth,
and says to it: "You're very bright and fair!
I've worn you at the royal court for years.
The emperor of France will never say
I died alone here in a foreign land
before their best men paid for you in full."
The pagans say: "Let's stop this bickering!"   *450*

« 35 »

The better Saracens prevail on him
till finally Marsilla takes his throne.
"You do us wrong," announces the caliph,°
"if you intend to strike this Frenchman here;
you ought to listen to him, hear him out."
"My lord," says Ganelon, "this I must suffer—
but I'll not fail, for all the gold God made,
or all the riches that are in this land,

---

453. This caliph may be the Omayyad usurper, Abdur Rahman
(see Introduction).

to tell him, if the time is given me,
460 the message Charles, the mighty king, sends him
by way of me—sends him, his mortal foe."
He wore a heavy mantle lined with sable
and covered in an Alexandrine silk.
He throws it down—it's caught by Blancandrin;
however, he will not give up his sword;
he keeps its golden hilt in his right hand.
The pagans all say: "Here's a noble baron!" AOI

« 36 »

Count Ganelon has come up to the king
and told him: "You are wrong to be incensed
470 when Charles, who governs France, thus sends you word
that you are to accept the Christian faith,
for he will give you half of Spain in fief—
his nephew Roland is to have the other—
you'll have a mighty boastful partner there!
If you will not comply with this accord,
in Saragossa you shall be besieged;
by force you shall be taken captive, bound,
transported straight to Aix, the capital.
You'll have there neither destrier nor palfrey
480 nor horse- nor mare-mule you may ride upon;
you'll be set down upon a worthless pack-horse.
Up there you'll be condemned to lose your head:
our emperor has sent you this dispatch."
He puts it in the right hand of the pagan.

« 37 »

Marsilla's face grew colorless with rage.
He breaks the seal and throws the wax aside
and scans the page, sees what is written there:
"Charles, who governs France, addressing me,
reminds me of the anger and the grief
490 occasioned by Basan and his brother Basil,
whose heads I took in the hills of Haltilie.
In order to indemnify my life,
I'll have to send my uncle, the caliph—

if I do not, he'll lose no love on me."
Marsilla's son spoke next; addressing him,
he tells the king: "This Ganelon spoke nonsense—
he's gone so far, it's wrong that he still lives.
Just give him up to me—I'll do him justice!"
When Ganelon heard this, he flashed his sword
and set his back against a pine-tree trunk.   *500*

« 38 »

The king has now withdrawn into an orchard,
has taken his best men along with him;
and Blancandrin, whose hair is gray, went there,
and Jurfaleu, who is his son and heir,
and his faithful friend and uncle, the caliph.
Now Blancandrin says: "Call the Frenchman here;
he promised me that he would help our cause."
At this the king says: "Go and bring him here."
So by the right hand he took Ganelon
and led him through the orchard to the king.   *510*
They there discuss details of lawless treason. AOI

« 39 »

"My fair lord Ganelon," Marsilla told him,
"I acted somewhat hastily toward you
when in my rage I made as if to strike you.
I swear to you that, by these sable pelts
(their trimming's worth five-hundred pounds of gold),
before tomorrow night I'll make amends."
And Ganelon replies: "I won't refuse it.
And if it please God, you'll be well rewarded!" AOI

« 40 »

Marsilla then says: "Ganelon, know truly   *520*
that in my heart I'm very fond of you.
I'd like to hear you talk of Charlemagne.
He's very old, and has outworn his time;
I know for sure he's lived two hundred years.

494. More diplomatic language; see note, v. 306.

His body's knocked about so many lands,
his bossy shield has caught so many blows,
he's pauperized so many wealthy kings—
when will he ever leave off making war?"
"He's not like that at all," says Ganelon.
530 "No man who ever sees and comes to know him
will fail to say the emperor is great.
I cannot praise or laud him to you so
that he will not have yet more worth and honor.
His mighty courage—who would itemize it?
God made such heroism shine in him
that he would rather die than fail his barons."

« 41 »

The pagan says: "I really am amazed
by Charlemagne, who is old and has gray hair.
He's lived two hundred years and more, I know;
540 his body, battered in so many lands,
has caught so many blows from spears and lances;
he has pauperized so many wealthy kings—
when will he ever leave off making war?"
"He won't," says Ganelon, "while his nephew lives;
no braver man is under heaven's hood—
his friend Olivier is dauntless, too.
The dozen peers Charles thinks so highly of
head up a van of twenty thousand knights.
Secure as Charles is, no man frightens him." AOI

« 42 »

550 The Saracen says: "I am much amazed
by Charlemagne, who is grizzled and white-haired.
I know for sure he's better than two hundred.
Through many countries he's gone conquering
and caught so many blows from good, sharp spears,
left many rich kings dead upon the field—
when will he ever tire of making war?"
"He won't," says Ganelon, "while Roland lives;
there's none so brave from here to the Orient.
His friend Olivier is valiant, too.
560 The dozen peers Charles holds in such esteem

head up the van of twenty-thousand Franks.
So safe is Charles, he fears no man alive." AOI

« 43 »

"My fair lord Ganelon," says King Marsilla,
"I have such men—you won't see any finer—
four hundred thousand horsemen at my call.
Can I give battle to the French and Charles?"
"For now, do nothing," answers Ganelon.
"You'd suffer heavy losses of your pagans;
forget such foolishness and cleave to wisdom.
Bestow such bounty on the emperor   570
that there will be no Frank left unamazed.
Because of twenty hostages you'll send him,
the king will make his way back to sweet France.
Behind him he will station his rear guard:
his nephew Roland will be there, I think,
and gallant, courteous Olivier.
These counts are dead, if someone will believe me.
Then Charles will see the fall of his great pride;
he'll have no heart to fight you any more." AOI

« 44 »

"My fair lord Ganelon," says King Marsilla,   580
"in just what way am I to kill Count Roland?"
Says Ganelon: "I'll tell you how precisely:
the king will reach the main pass at Sizer,
while having left his guard deployed behind him.
His nephew will be there, the rich Count Roland,
and Olivier, whom he relies on so.
They'll have a force of twenty thousand Franks.
Send out a hundred thousand of your pagans
to make the first assault upon them there.
The men from France will be thinned out and   590
   crippled—
I do not say your side will not have losses—
but nonetheless, attack them once again;
there'll be no way for Roland to escape.
And then you shall have done a knightly deed:
throughout your lifetime you'll have no more war.
   AOI

« 45 »

"If someone were to cause the death of Roland,
then Charles would lose the right arm from his body;
the awe-inspiring host would cease to be;
no more would Charles assemble such a force,
600 and Tere Majur° would then be left in peace."
On hearing this, Marsilla kissed his neck,
and then his treasures started to arrive.

« 46 »

Marsilla says: "There's one thing more to say,
since counsel has no value without trust—
just pledge me the betrayal of Count Roland."
Then Ganelon replies: "As you desire!"
Upon the relics in his sword Murgleis
he swore high treason and betrayed himself. AOI

« 47 »

A throne carved out of ivory stood there.
610 Marsilla orders that a book be brought—
the laws of Termagant and of Mohammed.
The Spanish Saracen has sworn thereon,
that should he find Count Roland in the guard,
with all his forces he will give him battle
and, if he can, make sure that he is killed.
And Ganelon says: "May your will be done!" AOI

« 48 »

A pagan, Valdabron, approached just then.
This man came forward, up to King Marsilla,
and, laughing brightly, said to Ganelon:
620 "Here, take this sword. No man has any better;
the hilts go better than a thousand mangons.°
I give you this for friendship's sake, fair lord,
so you will help us with the baron Roland:
make sure that we may find him in the guard."
"It shall be done," Count Ganelon replies.
And then they kissed upon the cheek and chin.

600. Tere Majur, the "Great Land," includes the whole Carolingian empire.
621. The hilt of his sword, formed of two halves soldered together, is worth more than a thousand gold coins.

« 49 »

A pagan, Climborin, came afterward,
and laughing brightly said to Ganelon:
"Here, take my casque—I've never seen a better—
and give us help against the marquis Roland, 630
by showing us a way to humble him."
"It shall be done," Count Ganelon replied.
And then they kissed upon the mouth and cheek.
   AOI

« 50 »

Queen Bramimonde came up that very moment:
"I love you dearly, sir," she tells the count,
"my lord and all his men respect you so.
I'm sending these two brooches to your wife;
fine work of jacinths,° amethysts, and gold,
they're worth far more than all the wealth of Rome.
Your emperor has none so beautiful." 640
Accepting them, he put them in his boots. AOI

« 51 »

The king calls in his treasurer, Malduit:
"The goods for Charles—is everything made ready?"
"Yes, sire, quite well," the man says. "Seven hundred
camels loaded down with gold and silver,
and the twenty noblest hostages on earth." AOI

« 52 »

The king clasped Ganelon about the shoulder
and said to him: "You're very brave and wise,
but by that law you hold to be most sacred,
be sure you never turn your heart from us. 650
I mean to give you vast sums of my wealth,
ten mule-loads of the best Arabian gold;
no year will pass but I shall do the same.
Accept the keys to this wide fortress town;
present this lavish tribute to King Charles—

638. *jacinth:* an ancient gemstone, possibly the sapphire.

get Roland put into the guard for me.
If I can find him in a pass or gorge,
then I shall give him battle to the death."
"I think I've stayed too long," says Ganelon.
660   He then mounts up and sets out on his way. AOI

« 53 »

The emperor, commencing his withdrawal,
has come into the fortress town of Galne;
Count Roland, he had captured it and razed it—
a hundred years hence it would still lie waste.
The king waits there for news from Ganelon
and tribute from the mighty land of Spain.
At dawn one morning, as the sky grew light,
Count Ganelon arrived at the encampment. AOI

« 54 »

The emperor has risen in the morning:
670   the king has heard his matins and his mass.
He stood upon green grass before his tent.
Roland was there, and brave Olivier,
as were Duke Naimes and many others, too.
False Ganelon the perjurer arrives.
With great adroitness he begins to speak,
and to the king he says: "Be saved by God!
I bring you here the keys of Saragossa;
immense and lavish gifts I bring to you,
and twenty hostages—keep them under guard.
680   Thereto brave King Marsilla sends you word
that you must not blame him for the caliph—
I saw, myself, four hundred thousand troops
in hauberks, some of them with helmets laced,
and swords strapped on, their pommels gold and niello,°
providing him safe conduct to the sea.
They left Marsilla, for the Christian law
they neither will receive nor recognize.
Before they had the time to sail four leagues,

684. *niello:* ornamental work consisting of a black sulphur-based alloy inlaid on a metal surface.

a high wind and a rainstorm caught them up
and drowned them there—you won't see them again.　*690*
If he had been alive, I would have brought him.
As for the pagan king, sire, rest assured,
before you see a single month go by,
he'll follow you into the realm of France
and there he will receive the faith you hold;
with clasped hands he will be at your command,
and by your leave will hold the realm of Spain."
At this the king says: "Thanks be unto God!
You've done well; you shall have a great reward."
Throughout the host a thousand trumpets sound;　*700*
the Franks break camp and get their pack-mules
　　loaded;
they all are on their way now to sweet France. AOI

« 55 »

Charlemagne has devastated Spain,
has seized its castles, ravaged its walled towns;
the king now says that his campaign is ended,
and toward sweet France the emperor rides out.
Count Roland has attached his battle pennant
and raised it skyward, high upon a hill;
throughout the countryside the Franks pitch camp.
The pagans ride down through the broader valleys,　*710*
their hauberks on and gorgets tightly shut,
their helmets laced, their swords upon their hips,
their shields hung from their necks, their lances pen-
　　noned.
They hold up in a thicket in the hills:
four hundred thousand wait for break of day.
Oh God! the French know nothing of all this! AOI

« 56 »

The day goes by, serenely evening falls,
and Charles, the mighty emperor, is sleeping.
He dreamed he'd reached the main pass at Sizer—
within his fist he held his ashwood lance—　*720*
Count Ganelon then yanked it from his grasp
and brandished it and smashed it with such rage

that splinters from it flew up to the sky.
And Charles sleeps on; he still does not wake up.

« 57 »

He dreams another vision after this:
he was in France, at Aix, within his chapel—
a vicious boar is biting his right arm.
He sees a leopard coming from Ardennes°
that furiously rips into his body.
730　Then down from his great hall a boar-hound came
　　and hurled himself toward Charles by leaps and
　　　　bounds.
He bit the right ear off the former beast—
infuriated, he attacked the leopard.
The Frenchmen say the battle was intense,
but cannot tell which one of them will win.
And Charles sleeps on; he still has not awakened. AOI

« 58 »

The night goes by and shining dawn appears:
throughout the host the sound of trumpets rings.
Imposingly, the emperor rides out.
740　Says Charles the emperor, "My lords and barons,
observe the narrow gorges and the gaps;
decide for me who'll stay with the rear guard."
"My stepson° Roland," Ganelon replies.
"You have no lord of such great vassalage."°
On hearing this, the king looks at him sharply
and answers him with, "You're a fiend incarnate.
A deadly rage has passed into your body.
—And who'll be out before me, in the van?"
"Oger of Denmark," answers Ganelon.
750　"You have no baron who can do it better."

728. *Ardennes:* ε large forest on the border of Belgium and
France.
743. Ganelon uses the word *fillastre* here, parodying Roland's
earlier *padrastre* (v. 277). Both terms are ambiguous, with overtones of insult; i.e., "poor excuse for a son/father."
744. *vassalage:* courage, fidelity, honesty, etc.—all the qualities
which go to make up the perfect vassal.

« 59 »

Count Roland, when he heard himself assigned, AOI
spoke out, adhering to chivalric code:
"My lord stepfather, I must hold you dear;
you've put the rear guard under my command!
There Charles, the king of France, shall never lose,
I know for sure, a destrier or palfrey
or horse- or mare-mule that is fit to ride,
nor will he even lose a nag or pack-horse
that has not first been purchased by the sword."
"I know," says Ganelon, "you've spoken truly." AOI   *760*

« 60 »

When Roland hears that he'll be in the guard,
he angrily addresses his stepsire:
"Ah, coward, you low-born, malicious slave,
did you believe I'd let the gauntlet fall
the way you did the staff in front of Charles?" AOI

« 61 »

"Just Emperor," begins the baron Roland,
"give me the bow° you're holding in your hand.
I know for certain I'll not be reproved
for having dropped it, as did Ganelon
from his right hand, when he received the staff."   *770*
The emperor, his head as yet inclined,
tugs gently at his beard, twists his moustache.
He cannot keep his eyes from shedding tears.

« 62 »

A moment later Naimes came up to them
(there was no finer vassal in the court)
and told the king: "You've listened well to this:
Count Roland, though he's very irritated,
has had the rear guard put in his command;
you have no baron who would alter that.
Confer on him the bow that you have bent   *780*

767. The bow is an emblem of military command.

and then find men for him who'll serve him well."
The king let go of it and Roland took it.

« 63 »

The emperor informs his nephew Roland:
"My fair lord nephew, know this for the truth:
I'm making you a gift of half my host.
Keep them intact, for that is your salvation."
At this the count says: "I'll do no such thing.
God blast me if I'll shame my family!
I'll keep back twenty thousand good, brave Franks;
790 you'll make it through the pass in perfect safety.
You need fear no one while I'm still alive!"

« 64 »

Count Roland climbed up on his destrier. AOI
Olivier, his comrade, comes to join him.
Gerin came there, and brave Count Gerier;
Aton° came there, and then came Berenger;°
Astor came there, and Anseïs the Proud;
there came Gerard of Roussillon the Elder;°
the rich Duke Gaifier° has come there, too.
The archbishop says: "And *I'll* go, by my head!"
800 "And I'm with you," then says Count Gautier,
"I'm Roland's man; I must not let him down."
They pick out twenty thousand chevaliers. AOI

« 65 »

Count Roland summons Gautier of Hum:
"You take a thousand Franks from France, our land,
and occupy the hilltops and ravines,
so the emperor won't lose a single man." AOI
"I'll do my best for you," says Gautier.

795–800. The names Aton and Berenger were both associated
with the Crusades; one Gerard of Roussillon was the hero of a
Provençal *chanson de geste* of the ninth century, and another was
a Crusader; Gaifier, a duke of Aquitaine, was first an enemy,
later a friend, of Charlemagne's father, and his name occurs frequently in medieval epic and romance; Gautier of Hum apparently does not exist outside the pages of the *Song of Roland*.

With a thousand Franks from France, their land,
    Gautier
rode forth to scout the hilltops and ravines.
However bad the news, he won't come down   810
till seven hundred swords have been unsheathed.
King Almaris from the kingdom of Belferne
will give him battle on that ghastly day.

« 66 »

The hills are high, the valleys deep in shade,
with dull brown cliffs and awe-inspiring gorges.
Today the Frenchmen are to know great pain.
Their clamor can be heard for fifteen leagues.
When finally they get to Tere Majur
and look on Gascony, their liege-lord's land,
their thoughts turn to their honors and their fiefs,   820
and to their sweethearts and their noble wives:
there's no one there who isn't moved to tears.
But Charles is anguished more than all the rest—
he has left his nephew in the Spanish passes.
And seized with grief, he cannot help but cry. AOI

« 67 »

The dozen peers have stayed behind in Spain,
with a company of twenty thousand Franks;
they're not afraid, and have no fear of death.
The emperor has gone back into France;
beneath his mantle, he conceals his face.   830
And when Duke Naimes comes riding up to him
and asks the king: "What's causing you such grief?"
Charles answers: "He who asks me that offends me.
I feel such grief, I cannot help lamenting,
for France will be destroyed by Ganelon.
Last night I had a vision sent by angels
in which he smashed the lance within my hands—
the man who picked my nephew for the guard.
I've left him out there in a hostile land—
Oh God! If he is lost, I can't replace him." AOI   840

« 68 »

Charlemagne can't help himself; he weeps.
A hundred thousand Franks feel grief for him
and a curious anxiety for Roland.
The villain Ganelon has done his treason,
accepted lavish gifts from the pagan king
of gold and silver, silken cloaks, brocades,
of horses and horse-mules, and lions and camels.
Marsilla summons up his Spanish barons
and counts, viscounts, and dukes and almaçors°
850   and chieftains, and the sons of his contors;°
in three days' time he has four hundred thousand.
He lets his drums resound through Saragossa;
they raise Mohammed to the highest tower—
no pagan fails to praise and worship him.
They ride out then, by grueling forced marches
across the peaks and valleys of Certaine;
they spot the pennants of the men from France.
The guard, commanded by the twelve companions,
do not intend to shy away from battle.

« 69 »

860   The nephew of Marsilla has come forward
upon a mule he pokes at with a stick.
In a clear and laughing voice he tells his uncle:
"Fair sire, my king, I've served you for so long;
for salary I've suffered pain and torment,
fought battles and prevailed upon the field!
Give me a fief; that is, first crack at Roland,°
and I shall kill him with my sharpened spear.
Provided that Mohammed will protect me,
I'll set free every bit of land in Spain
870   from the Spanish passes down to Durestant.
     Then Charles will tire, and his Franks will have to
         yield.

849. *almaçor:* (Arab. *al mansûr,* "the victorious"), an eponym given a tenth-century regent of the Caliphate who led 56 campaigns against the Christians.
850. *contor:* a rank just below that of count.
866. To be given the first blow (*premier colp*) in battle was considered a special honor by Christians and pagans alike.

Throughout your lifetime, you'll have no more war."
The king Marsilla handed him the glove. AOI

« 70 »

The glove still in his fist, Marsilla's nephew
appeals in fiery language to his uncle:
"You've given me a priceless gift, fair sire;
now pick me out a dozen of your lords,
so I may go combat the twelve companions."
The first of all to speak was Falsaron
(this man was brother to the king Marsilla):   880
"My fair lord nephew, you and I shall go,
and we will give them battle, without fail.
The rear guard of the mighty host of Charles—
it's foreordained that we shall slaughter them." AOI

« 71 »

King Corsablis is standing not far off.
From Barbary, an expert at black magic,
this man has spoken as a vassal should;
for all God's gold he wouldn't be a coward.
But look: Malprimis of Brigant spurs up—
he's faster on his feet than any horse.   890
Before Marsilla this man shrilly yells:
"I'll go and take myself to Roncesvals:
if I find Roland there, I'll lay him low!"

« 72 »

From Balaguer a chieftain has arrived.
Superbly built, with savage, clean-cut features,
whenever he is mounted on his horse,
he bears his weapons with a dauntless air;
and, celebrated for his vassalage,
he'd be a rightful lord, were he a Christian.
Before Marsilla, this man thundered out: 900
"I'll gamble with myself at Roncesvals!
If I find Roland there, he's dead and gone,
and Olivier, and all the dozen peers.
The French will die in sorrow and disgrace.
Since Charlemagne is old and doddering,
he'll change his attitude toward waging war,

and Spain will then be left to us in peace."
The king Marsilla thanked him very much. AOI

« 73 »

An almaçor is there from Moriane;°
910 no viler man is in the land of Spain.
Before Marsilla he has made his vaunt:
"I'll lead my company to Roncesvals,
all twenty thousand men, with shields and lances.
If I find Roland there, I swear he's dead.
The day will never come that Charles won't mourn."
    AOI

« 74 »

Not far off stands Turgis of Tortelose:°
this man's a count; the town is therefore his.
He has vowed undying hatred toward the Christians.
He falls in with the rest before Marsilla,
920 announcing to the king: "Do not despair!
Mohammed's worth far more than Rome's Saint
        Peter—
serve him, and honors of the field are ours.
I'll go meet Roland there at Roncesvals;
he'll have no one to keep him safe from death.
Look at my sword, how fine and long it is:
I'll measure it against his Durendal,
and soon enough you'll hear which one prevailed.
If they come out to us, the French will die.
Old Charles will know both sorrow and disgrace,
930 and nevermore on earth will wear a crown."

« 75 »

Not far away is Escremiz of Valterne:
that land is his, for he's a Saracen.
He calls out from the crowd before Marsilla:
"I'll go to Roncesvals and crush their pride!
If I find Roland, he shall have no head,

909. *Moriane:* probably Moriana on the Ebro, a town on the
pilgrimage route to Santiago.
916. *Tortelose:* a town on the Ebro in Catalonia.

nor shall Olivier, who leads the others.
The dozen peers have all been marked for death;
the French will die and France will be diminished,
and Charles will have a shortage of good men." AOI

« 76 »

Not far off stands a pagan, Esturgant;　　940
Estramariz, a comrade, stands there, too:
these men are evil, treacherous deceivers.
Marsilla now speaks out: "My lords, advance!
At Roncesvals you'll go through the ravines
and help with the direction of my troops."
And these men answer him: "At your command!
Olivier and Roland we'll attack,
nor shall the dozen peers be saved from death.
These swords of ours are finely made and sharp;
with hot blood we shall soon vermillion them.　　950
The French will die; King Charles will be distressed,
and we'll make you a gift of Tere Majur.
If you really want to see this, king, come on,
and we shall give the emperor to you."

« 77 »

Now Margariz° of Seville came dashing up;
he rules that land as far as Cazmarine.°
He's loved by all the ladies, he's so handsome;
not one can look his way without a glow,
nor, looking at him, keep herself from giggling.
No other pagan is so chivalrous.　　960
He joined the crowd, called out above the rest,
proclaiming to the king: "Do not despair!
I'll go to Roncesvals and finish Roland,
nor will Olivier leave there alive.
The dozen peers are doomed to martyrdom.
You see my sword, whose hilt is made of gold,
presented me by the great emir of Primes—
I swear it shall be plunged in crimson blood.
The French will die, and France will be disgraced,
and ancient Charles, whose beard is shot with white,　　970

955. *Margariz:* a Byzantine word meaning "renegade."
956. Cazmarine is probably Camariñas, in the province of Galicia.

won't see the day he feels no grief or anger.
Within a year's time we'll have conquered France;
we'll take our ease in the town of Saint-Denis."°
The pagan king made him a sweeping bow.° AOI

« 78 »

Chernuble of Munigre° stands nearby:
his flowing hair sweeps down along the ground.
While playing, he will lift more weight for fun
than four pack-mules can carry, fully loaded.
It's said that in the land from which he comes
980   no sunlight shines, the wheat cannot mature,
no rain falls, and there's never been a dew;
no rock is there that isn't solid black—
some say it is the devils' habitation.
Chernuble says: "I've strapped on my good sword;
I'll tint it crimson there at Roncesvals,
and if I find proud Roland in my path
and don't attack him, take my word no more;
and I shall conquer Durendal with mine.
The French will die, and France will be diminished."
990   And at these words the twelve peers come together.
They lead a hundred thousand Saracens,
who scramble forward, eager for a battle.
Beneath a grove of pines they arm themselves.

« 79 »

The pagans put on Saracen-style hauberks,
the bulk of them of triple-thickness mail,
lace up their well-made Saragossan helmets,
and gird themselves with swords of Viennois° steel;
they carry handsome shields, Valencian° spears,
and blue and white and crimson battle flags.
1000   They leave behind the mules and all the palfreys
and, mounting destriers, ride out in ranks.

---

973. *the town of Saint-Denis:* Paris.
975. *Munigre:* possibly the desolate region of Los Monegros, east
of Saragossa.
997–98. Vienne, on the Rhône in France, and Valencia, in eastern
Spain, were both famous for their armories.

The day was bright, the sunshine beautiful;
no piece of armor failed to catch the light.
A thousand trumpets sing, to add more splendor;
so deafening their noise, the Frenchmen hear it.
"My lord companion," says Olivier,
"I think we'll have some Saracens to fight."
And Roland answers: "Grant us this, oh God!
It's fitting we should stay here for our king:
a man should suffer hardships for his lord,   *1010*
and persevere in fearful heat and cold;
a man should lose, if need be, hide and hair.
Now each of you be sure to strike hard blows,
so mocking songs may not be sung of us!
The pagan cause is wrong, the Christian right:
I won't be made into a bad example." AOI

« 80 »

Olivier has climbed to higher ground,
looks down a grassy valley to his right,
and sees that pagan horde approaching them.
He calls out then to Roland, his companion: *1020*
"From Spain I see a dreadful glare approaching,
so many shiny hauberks, blazing casques!
They'll cause us French enormous suffering.
That fraud, that traitor Ganelon knew this,
appointing us before the emperor."
"Olivier, be quiet," Roland answers,
"I'll hear not one word more, for he's my stepsire."

« 81 »

Olivier climbs up to higher ground
and takes a good look at the Spanish realm
and at the horde of Saracens assembled: *1030*
those helmets, set with gems and gold, flash light,
as do those shields and saffron-yellow hauberks,
those lances and those furled-up battle flags.
He cannot even add up the battalions—
there are so many there he loses count—
and privately he feels quite disconcerted.
At breakneck speed he came down off the hill,
approached the French, and told them everything.

« 82 »

"I've seen the pagans," says Olivier,
1040 "no man on earth has ever seen so many—
at least a hundred thousand in the van,
with shields, and helmets laced, and shining hauberks,
and lances raised, their burnished tips aglow.
You'll have a battle such as never was.
Oh, lords of France, may you have strength from God
to hold the field, so we shall not be beaten!"
The French say: "Damn the man who runs away!
Not one of us will fail you, unto death." AOI

« 83 »

Olivier says: "There are many pagans,
1050 and, it seems to me, we Franks are few.
Companion Roland, you should sound your horn,°
so Charles will hear and bring the army back."
Count Roland answers: "I would play the fool!
throughout sweet France my glory would be lost.
I'll soon strike mighty blows with Durendal,
until its blade is bloody to the gold.
These pagans err in coming to the pass;
I promise you, they all are marked for death." AOI

« 84 »

"Companion Roland, sound the oliphant,
1060 so Charles will hear and bring his army back;
the king, with all his lords, will rescue us."
But Roland says: "Almighty God forbid
my family should be reproved for me,
or sweet France ever fall into disgrace!
Instead I'll lay on so with Durendal,
the good sword I have strapped upon my hip,
that you shall see its blade all drenched with blood.
The pagans have assembled to their sorrow:
I promise you, they all are marked for death." AOI

1051. *your horn:* Roland's famous *oliphant,* made from an elephant's tusk.

« 85 »

"Companion Roland, sound your oliphant,   1070
so Charles, who's going through the pass, will hear;
I promise you, the Franks will soon return."
"May God forbid," flung Roland back at him,
"that it be said by any man alive
I ever blew my horn because of pagans!
My family shall never be reproved.
When I am in the midst of this great battle
and strike a thousand blows, then seven hundred,
you'll see the blade of Durendal run blood.
The French are good; they'll fight with vassalage;   1080
the men from Spain will not be saved from death."

« 86 »

"I see no fault here," says Olivier,
"for I have seen the Saracens from Spain:
they swarm upon the mountains and the valleys,
along the hillsides, and throughout the plains.
The army of these foreigners is large,
and we have but a little company."
"This makes me still more eager," Roland says,
"Almighty God forbid, and all His angels,
that France should lose her fame because of me!   1090
I'd much prefer to die than come to shame;
for fighting well, the emperor will love us."

« 87 »

Roland is bold, Olivier is wise,
and both of them are marvelously brave.
When they are armed and mounted on their horses,
not even death can make them shy from battle;
these counts are worthy men, their speech is proud.
The vicious pagans ride on in great fury.
Olivier says: "Roland, look at them;
they're close to us, but Charles is now too far.   1100
You wouldn't deign to sound your ivory horn:
but were the king here, we would be unharmed.
Just take a look up toward the Spanish pass;

you there can see the desolate rear guard;
the men in it will never form another."
"Don't talk such nonsense!" Roland answers him.
"The heart that quavers in the breast be damned!
We'll stand our ground right here upon the field;
here *we'll* provide the carnage and the slaughter."
　　AOI

« 88 »

1110 When Roland sees that there will be a battle,
he is fiercer than a leopard or a lion.
He hails the Franks, then calls Olivier:
"My lord companion, friend, don't talk that way!
The emperor, who left these Franks with us—
some twenty thousand of them he detached—
made sure there was no coward in the lot.
A man should suffer hardships for his lord,
and persevere through dreadful heat and cold;
a man should lose, if need be, flesh and blood.
1120 So ply your lance, as I shall Durendal,
my well-made sword the king once gave to me.
If I should die here, then whoever gets it
can say a noble vassal owned it once."

« 89 »

Not far away is Turpin, the archbishop:
he spurs his horse and rides up on a knoll;
he calls the French, delivers them a sermon:
"My lords and barons, Charles has left us here,
and we must die, if need be, for our king.
You now must help sustain the Christian faith.
1130 You'll have a battle, rest assured of that—
before your eyes you see the Saracens.
Confess your sins, and pray to God for mercy;
to save your souls, I'll give you absolution.
If then you die, you'll all be holy martyrs
and take your seats in highest Paradise."
The French dismount and kneel upon the ground;
in God's name the archbishop blesses them:
as penance he commands that they go fight.

« 90 »

The Frenchmen rise and get upon their feet:
they now are well absolved and freed from sin   *1140*
and blessed by the archbishop in God's name.
This done, they mount their prancing destriers.
They all have been equipped in knightly fashion
and properly outfitted for the battle.
Count Roland comments to Olivier:
"My lord companion, you knew very well
that Ganelon had victimized us all.
He has taken gold and wealth and deniers;°
the emperor must now avenge us well!
Though King Marsilla got us in a bargain,   *1150*
he still will have to close the deal with swords!" AOI

« 91 »

Count Roland rode into the Spanish pass
on Veillantif, his good, fast-gaited horse:
the armor that he wears becomes him well.
The baron rides forth, brandishing his lance:
its upraised ferrule moves against the sky,
a pure white pennant laced upon its shaft,
whose golden fringes flutter at his hands.
He is well built, his features frank and smiling;
his comrade comes along, not far behind: *1160*
the men from France consider him their champion.
He gazes fiercely toward the Saracens,
engagingly and humbly toward the French,
then courteously says a word to them:
"My lords and barons, gently, at a walk!
These pagans have come looking for a slaughter;
before night falls we'll take fine, handsome plunder,
the likes of which no French king ever owned."
And at these words the armies come together. AOI

1148. *denier:* a small silver coin in use throughout Western Europe
up to the time of the French Revolution. It is used later on in
the *Song of Roland* as a metonym denoting little value; i.e., "not
worth a denier."

« 92 »

1170 Olivier says: "I've no heart for words.
      You neither deigned to sound your ivory horn,
      nor wanted any help at all from Charles.
      It's not that brave man's fault, for he knows nothing,
      nor may those here be blamed in any way.
      So go ahead and ride for all you're worth.
      —My lords and barons, hold the battlefield!
      I beg of you, for God's sake be resolved
      to strike, and give as well as you receive!
      Let's not forget the battle cry of Charles."
1180 And with this word the Frenchmen raised the cry.
      Whoever might have heard them shout "Monjoy!"°
      would be reminded of their vassalage.
      And then they ride!—my God, with such defiance!
      They spur to make their horses run all out,
      and go to strike—what else are they to do?
      The Saracens are not at all afraid.
      Now look: the pagans and the Franks engage.

« 93 »

      Marsilla's nephew (Aëlroth was his name)
      rides well out in advance of all the host,
1190 goes shouting words of insult to our French:
      "French villains, you shall fight with us today,
      for he who should protect you has betrayed you;
      the king who left you in this pass is mad.
      This very day sweet France shall lose her fame,
      and Charlemagne the right arm from his body."°
      When Roland hears this, God! is he enraged!
      He spurs his horse and lets him run all out
      and goes to strike the count with all his force;

1181. Monjoy ("joyous mountain") is Charlemagne's battle cry.
Several theories have been advanced to explain its origin: (1) a
mound of stones set up to mark the site of a victory was called a
montjoie, and the Carolingian battle cry referred specifically to
the one celebrating the martyrdom of Saint-Denis; and (2) the
name Monte Gaudia was given the hill from which pilgrims got
their first glimpse of the holy city of Rome. Even the author of
the Song of Roland has a theory about the word (see verses
3093–95).
1195. I.e., Roland.

he breaks his shield and lays his hauberk open
and pierces through his chest and cracks the bones   *1200*
and cuts the spine completely from the back
and with his lance casts out his mortal soul,
impales him well, and hoists the body up
and throws him dead a spear's length from his horse.
The neck-bone has been broken into halves,
and still he does not leave, but tells him this:
"You utter coward, Charles is not a fool,
nor has he ever had a love of treason.
His act was brave, to leave us at the pass;
today sweet France is not to lose her fame.   *1210*
Now lay on, Franks! the first blow has been ours.
We're in the right, these gluttons in the wrong!" AOI

« 94 »

A duke is there whose name is Falsaron:
this man was brother to the king Marsilla
and held the land of Abiram and Dathan.°
Beneath the sky there is no fouler villain;
between the eyes, his forehead is enormous—
a half-foot wide, were one to measure it.
He's furious to see his nephew dead,
and leaves the ranks to fly at anyone,   *1220*
while bellowing the pagan battle cry:
his hatred for the Frenchmen is immense.
"This very day sweet France will lose her honor!"
Olivier hears this and is enraged.
He digs his golden spurs into his horse
and goes to fight him in a knightly manner:
he breaks his shield and smashes through his hauberk
and drives his pennant's fringe into his body.
He throws him dead a spear's length from his saddle,
looks down and sees the glutton lying there,   *1230*
and then addresses him defiantly:
"Your blustering does not disturb me, coward.
—Now lay on, Franks, for we shall whip them well.
Monjoy!" He roars out Charles's battle cry. AOI

1215. *Abiram and Dathan:* rebels against Moses in the wilderness
of Paran.

« 95 »

A king was there whose name is Corsablis.
He comes from Barbary, a distant land:
he called out to the other Saracens:
"We ought to win this battle easily.
Because the Frankish force is very small,
1240 for those few here we only have contempt.
Not one of them will be reprieved by Charles;
the day has come when they shall have to die."
Archbishop Turpin overheard this well:
he hates no man beneath the sky so much.
He rakes his horse with spurs of finest gold,
and rides to the attack with all his might.
He breaks his shield, demolishes his hauberk,
and drives his great lance deep into his body,
impales him well, then hoists the dead man up
1250 and throws the corpse a spear's length down the road.
He glances back, observes the glutton there,
and does not leave until he says these words:
"You turntail pagan, you have told a lie!
King Charles, my lord, will always be our champion;
we Frenchmen have no wish to run away.
We'll give all your companions their quietus;
I've news for you—you're just about to die.
Now lay on, Franks! Remember who you are!
Give thanks to God, the first blow has been ours.
1260 "Monjoy!" he shouts, so they will hold the field.

« 96 »

Gerin attacks Malprimis of Brigal.
His fine shield isn't worth a denier;
its crystal boss is totally demolished
and half of it falls down upon the ground.
He rips his hauberk open to the flesh
and plunges his good lance into his body.
The pagan topples over in a heap,
and Satan comes and carries off his soul. AOI

« 97 »

Next Gerier, his comrade, strikes the chieftain.
He breaks his shield, tears loose his hauberk's mail,   *1270*
and puts his well-made lance into his entrails,
impales him well, completely through the body,
and throws the corpse to earth a spear's length off.
"A splendid battle!" says Olivier.

« 98 »

The duke Sanson attacks the almaçor.
He breaks his gilt, fleuron-emblazoned shield—
the well-made hauberk gives him no protection—
and cuts him to the liver, lights, and heart,
then willy-nilly throws the man down dead.
The archbishop says: "A baron struck that blow!"   *1280*

« 99 »

Next Anseïs allows his horse to run,
and goes to strike Turgis of Tortelose.
He breaks his shield beneath its golden boss,
tears through the double thickness of his hauberk,
then puts his good spear's head into his body,
impales him well and drives the steel clear through
and tumbles him to earth a spear's length off.
Then Roland says: "A hero struck that blow!"

« 100 »

And Engeller, the Gascon from Bordeaux,
first spurs his horse, then, slackening his rein,   *1290*
goes out to fight with Escremiz of Valterne.
He cracks his shield and knocks it from his neck
and rips into his hauberk at the gorget
and hits his throat between the collarbones;
he throws the corpse a spear's length from the saddle,
and tells him afterward: "Now you're in hell!" AOI

« 101 »

Aton then hits a pagan, Esturgant,
upon the upper border of his shield,

cuts down clear through the crimson and the white;
1300 he rips into the skirting of his hauberk
and drives his good, sharp lance into his body,
then throws the corpse down off his prancing horse.
He tells him afterward: "You won't be saved!"

« 102 »

And Berenger attacks Estramariz.
He breaks his shield, demolishes his hauberk,
then spits him on his sturdy lance and throws
the corpse among a thousand Saracens.
Among the twelve peers, ten have been dispatched;
no more than two of them are still alive:
1310 Chernuble and the count called Margariz.

« 103 »

Count Margariz is a very gallant knight—
good-looking, powerful, agile, and quick.
He spurs his horse, attacks Olivier.
He breaks his shield beneath its golden boss,
and runs his lancehead down along his side,
but God protects his body; he's untouched.
The lance-shaft breaks; however, he's not thrown.
He° rides on through, for no one tries to stop him,
and sounds his trumpet, rallying his men.

« 104 »

1320 The battle rages, spreads throughout the hosts:
Count Roland pays no heed to his own safety,
but plies his lance as long as its shaft holds—
with fifteen blows it's splintered and is useless—
and then unsheathes his good sword Durendal.
He spurs his horse and goes against Chernuble:
he breaks the helmet on which rubies° gleam;
he slices downward through the coif and hair

1318. *he:* Margariz.
1326. *rubies:* The word *carboncle* was used to designate any of
several red gemstones, including the ruby and the garnet. It was
thought that these stones gave off their own light.

and cuts between the eyes, down through his face,
the shiny hauberk made of fine-linked mail,
entirely through the torso to the groin, 1330
and through the saddle trimmed with beaten gold.
The body of the horse slows down the sword,
which, seeking out no joint, divides the spine:
both fall down dead upon the field's thick grass.
He says then: "Coward, you have come in vain!
Mohammed will not give you any help;
no glutton such as you will win this fight."

« 105 »

Count Roland gallops through the battlefield
with slicing, cleaving Durendal in hand:
he plays great havoc with the Saracens. 1340
Could you but see him piling corpse on corpse,
while pools of bright blood spread out on the ground!
His hauberk's drenched with gore, and both his arms,
the withers and the neck of his good horse.
Olivier does not decline to fight,
nor will the twelve peers need to be reproached,
nor all the French who fight and slaughter there.
The pagans die, and many of them faint.
The archbishop says: "A blessing on our barons!"
and shouts "Monjoy!"—the battle cry of Charles. AOI 1350

« 106 »

Olivier now gallops through the fray—
his lance has snapped, he only has a stump—
and goes to strike a pagan, Malsaron.
He breaks his gilt, fleuron-emblazoned shield,
bursting both his eyeballs from his head—
his brain comes tumbling downward to his feet—
then piles the corpse on seven hundred more.
He later killed Turgis and Esturgoz.
His lance is smashed and splintered to the grip,
and Roland says: "Companion, what are you doing? 1360
I wouldn't want a stick in such a battle;
here iron and steel are worth a great deal more.
Where is your sword, whose name is Halteclere?

Its hilt is made of gold, its pommel crystal."
Olivier replies: "I couldn't draw it;
I've been so occupied today with fighting." AOI

« 107 »

Olivier now drew his well-made sword,
as his companion Roland urged him to,
saluting him in proper knightly fashion.
1370 He strikes Justin of Val-Ferée, a pagan;
he slashes through the center of his head
and cleaves the trunk, the saffron-yellow byrnie,
the well-made saddle set with gems and gold,
and slices through the backbone of the horse;
both fall down dead before him on the field.
Then Roland tells him: "*Now* I know you, brother;
for blows like these the emperor will love us."
And on all sides the cry "Monjoy!" is raised. AOI

« 108 »

Gerin is mounted on his horse called Sorrel,
1380 his comrade Gerier on Passecerf:
they slacken rein, both dig in with their spurs,
and go to strike a pagan, Timozel,
one on the shield, the other on the hauberk.
Their lances both break off within his body;
they pitch the corpse into a fallow field.
I've neither heard it said, nor do I know
which vassal of the two was more courageous.

. . . °
. . . °

1390 The archbishop helps them, killing Siglorel,
the black magician who was once in Hell,
led there through magic spells by Jupiter.
Then Turpin says: "This one was meant for us."
"The coward has been vanquished," answers Roland.
"A lovely stroke, Olivier my brother!"

1388–89. These two lines are illegible.
1390. Siglorel, a prototype of Merlin, is unknown beyond this
reference.

« 109 »

The fighting, meanwhile, has become more savage.
The Franks and pagans strike prodigious blows;
one side attacks, the other holds its ground.
So many spear-shafts there are split and bloody,
so many battle flags and pennants torn!   *1400*
So many splendid Franks give up their youth!
They'll never see their mothers nor their wives,
nor the Frenchmen who await them at the pass.
Though Charlemagne may weep and mourn for them,
what difference does it make? They won't be helped.
Count Ganelon served evilly that day
he sold his people° out in Saragossa.
He lost both life and limb because of that,
by trial at Aix was sentenced to be hanged,
together with some thirty of his kin   *1410*
who never contemplated such a death. AOI

« 110 »

The battle is incredible and grim.
Olivier and Roland fight quite well,
the archbishop strikes a thousand blows and more,
the dozen peers do not let up a bit;
the Frenchmen who are there all fight together.
By hundreds and by thousands, pagans die;
no one who doesn't flee is safe from death—
like it or not, their time has all run out.
The Frenchmen lose their finest ornaments: *1420*
they'll never see their fathers nor their kin,
nor Charlemagne, who awaits them at the pass.
In France there is a very awesome tempest,
a raging storm of thunder, of high winds,
of rainfall, and of hail beyond all measure.
The thunderbolts crash down repeatedly—
in fact, there is a trembling of the earth.
From Saint Michael of the Peril° down to Seinz,°

1407. *people:* OF *maisnee*, the members of Charles's immediate household.
1428–29. For Mont Saint-Michel, see v. 152, n. Seinz is probably the modern Sens, a city Southeast of Paris. Besançon is a city in eastern France, near the Swiss border. Guitsand (Wissant) was a port on the English Channel.

from Besançon° to the harbor of Guitsand,°
1430 no house remains whose walls have not been cracked.
Around midday a widespread darkness falls,
and light comes only when the skies are torn.
No one can witness this without great fear,
and many say: "It is the final judgment—
the end of all Creation is at hand."
They do not know, nor do they speak the truth:
it is the requiem for Roland's death.

« 111 »

The French there fought with grit and resolution:
the pagans died by thousands and in swarms;
1440 of a hundred thousand, less than two survive.
The archbishop says: "Our men are very brave;
no man beneath the sky has any finer.
It is written in the *Annals of the Franks*°
that gallant fighters serve our emperor."
They go throughout the field to seek their own:
their eyes weep tears of tenderness and grief
and sorrow for their kinsmen, whom they loved.
Marsilla and his host rise up before them. AOI

« 112 »

Marsilla is advancing through a valley,
1450 together with the great host he assembled;
the king has numbered them in twenty columns.
Light flashes from those golden-studded casques
and from those shields and saffron-yellow byrnies.
Now seven thousand trumpets sound the charge:
the din is great throughout the countryside.
"Olivier, friend, brother," Roland says,
"false Ganelon has sentenced us to die;
his treason can no longer be concealed;
the emperor will have revenge for this.
1460 We'll have a bitter, hard-fought battle here,
the likes of which no man has ever seen.

1443. *Annals of the Franks* (OF *Geste Francor*) can refer to any
or all of the Latin histories written in the early Middle Ages about
the deeds of Charlemagne and his followers.

I'll strike them down with Durendal, my sword,
and you, companion, strike with Halteclere.
So many places we have carried them!
So many battles they have seen us through!
They won't become the theme of mocking songs."
　　AOI

« 113 »

Marsilla sees the slaughter of his men
and orders horns and trumpets to be sounded,
then rides out with his huge conscripted army.
Before them rides a Saracen, Abisme:　　*1470*
in all the troop there was no fouler man—
defiled by heinous crimes and evil deeds,
he doesn't trust in God, Saint Mary's son.
This man is just as black as molten pitch,
and treachery and murder he prefers
to having all the gold that's in Galicia.°
No man has ever seen him laugh or play,
yet he is very reckless and defiant:
for this he's wicked King Marsilla's pet.
He bears the dragon° rallying his men.　　*1480*
The archbishop never will be fond of him.
On seeing him, he feels an urge to fight,
and very quietly he tells himself:
"This Saracen's a heretic, I think.
It's best by far that I should go and kill him;
I've never cared for cowardice or cowards." AOI

« 114 »

The combat is begun by the archbishop:
he sits the horse he captured from Grossaille
(this was a king whom he had killed in Denmark).
The destrier is swift and full of spirit,　　*1490*
his hooves are cupped, his legs are smooth and flat,
his thighs are short, his crupper's very broad,
his back is high and straight, his body long,

1476. Especially the gold at the shrine of Saint James of Compostela.
1480. *the dragon:* Marsilla's ensign.

his mane is yellowish, his tail is white,
his ears are small, his head all golden brown:
no animal at all can run with him.
The archbishop spurs him on so valiantly,
not letting up till he accosts Abisme.
He goes and strikes him on his splendid shield.
1500 Inlaid with gems—topazes, amethysts,
esterminals,° and rubies blazing light—
it came from Val-Metas, a devil's gift;
Emir Galafe gave it in turn to him.
But Turpin strikes, not sparing it at all,
and now it's only worth a denier.
He spits his body through from side to side
and throws him dead upon an open spot.
The Frenchmen all say: "Here's a valiant man!
Salvation lies in our archbishop's crook."°

« 115 »

1510 The Frenchmen now can see how many pagans
have swarmed upon the field from everywhere:
they often call Olivier and Roland
and the dozen peers to furnish them protection.
The archbishop tells them what is on his mind:
"My lords and barons, don't think shameful thoughts!
I beg of you, for God's sake do not run,
nor let proud men sing mockingly of you;
it's best by far that we should die in combat.
Quite soon we are to meet our promised end;
1520 we won't remain alive beyond today;
however, I assure you of one thing:
that holy Paradise stands there for you,
and you'll be seated near the Innocents."
The Franks are so elated by these words,
that none among them fails to shout "Monjoy!" AOI

« 116 »

A Saracen was there from Saragossa
who held in his possession half the town;

1501. *esterminal:* an unidentified gemstone.
1509. *archbishop's crook:* that is, his lance.

this Climborin was not a man of honor.
He took an oath of faith with Ganelon
and kissed him on the mouth in amity   1530
and then gave him his ruby and his casque.
He'll bring disgrace on Tere Majur, he says,
and from the emperor will seize the crown.
He sits astride a horse called Barbamusche,
who is swifter than a sparrow hawk or swallow;
he spurs him briskly, slackening his rein,
and rides on Engelier of Gascony.
His shield and byrnie offer no defense;
he shoves his lance-head deep into his trunk,
impales him well, and drives the steel clear through.   1540
He throws him dead to earth a spear's length off,
then bellows: "They are ours for the taking;
so lay on, pagans, open up their ranks."
The French say: "God! so brave a knight to lose!"
    AOI

« 117 »

Count Roland calls Olivier aside:
"My lord companion, Engelier is dead;
we never had a more courageous knight."
The count replies: "May God let me avenge him!"
He rakes his horse with spurs of beaten gold,
grasps Halteclere, whose steel is drenched with blood;   1550
with all his might he goes and strikes the pagan,
twists free, and lets the Saracen fall down.
The Adversary carries off his soul.
And afterward he killed Duke Alphaïen,
and then he cut off Escabahi's head,
unseated seven Arabs from their horses—
they'll never have the nerve to fight again.
Count Roland says: "My comrade, when he's angry,
fights well enough to be compared to me;
for such strokes Charles will love us all the more."   1560
His voice rings out: "Lay on there, chevaliers!" AOI

« 118 »

A pagan, Valdabron, stands not far off:
this man it was who brought up King Marsilla.

At sea he can command four hundred dromonds,°
and not a skipper isn't sworn to him.
By treachery he took Jerusalem,
defiled the holy church of Solomon,
and killed the patriarch before the font.
This man, with whom Count Ganelon swore faith,
1570 gave him a thousand mangons and his sword.
He sits astride the horse called Gramimond,
who moves more rapidly than any falcon.
He rakes him briskly with his pointed spurs
and goes to strike the wealthy Duke Sanson:
he breaks his shield and smashes through his hauberk
and drives the pennant's fringe into his trunk,
then throws him dead a spear's length from his saddle.
"Now lay on, pagans; we shall whip them well!"
"O God!" the Franks say, "what a lord to lose!" AOI

« 119 »

1580 Count Roland, when he saw Sanson was dead,
was bitterly chagrined, as you might guess.
He spurs his horse to make him run all out.
With Durendal, that's worth its weight in gold,
the baron goes and strikes with all his force
upon the jewel-studded golden casque,
cuts downward through the head, the trunk and byrnie,
the well-made saddle set with gems and gold,
and deep into the backbone of the horse,
and to his shame or credit, kills them both.
1590 The pagans say: "That blow was hard on us!"
"I cannot love your kind," replies Count Roland.
"Your way is that of heresy and pride." AOI

« 120 »

From Africa there came an African
called Malquiant, the son of King Malcud.
His arms and armor, all of gold inlay,
above all others' flash against the sky.

1564. *dromonds:* large, fast sailing vessels of Greek origin, used chiefly as transports.

He sits astride the horse called Saut-Perdu;
no animal alive can run with him.
He goes and strikes the shield of Anseïs
and pierces through the crimson and the blue;   *1600*
he rips into the skirting of his hauberk
and drives both iron and wood into his body.
The count is dead; his time has all run out.
The French say: "Noble lord, you've come to grief!"

« 121 »

Archbishop Turpin goes throughout the field.
No tonsured priest who ever sang a mass
performed such feats of prowess with his body.
"God send you every ill," he tells the pagan.
"My heart laments your killing such a man,"
and making his good destrier plunge forward,   *1610*
belabored him on his Toledo shield,
then throws the dead man down upon green grass.

« 122 »

A pagan stands not far away, Grandoine,
King Capuel of Cappadocia's° son.
He sits astride the horse he calls Marmoire,
who is swifter than a bird upon the wing.
He slackens rein, he rakes him with his spurs,
and goes to strike Gerin with all his might.
He breaks the crimson shield about his neck,
and after that he opens up his byrnie   *1620*
and buries in his trunk his bright blue pennant,
then throws the corpse upon a high rock ledge.
He kills his comrade Gerier as well,
and Berenger and Guy of Saint-Antoine,°
then goes and strikes a wealthy duke, Astor,
who rules Envers-on-Rhône and Valérie:
he throws this man down dead; the pagans cheer.
"Our side is badly weakened," say the French.

1614. Cappadocia was an ancient Roman province in eastern Asia
Minor.
1624. *Saint-Antoine:* probably a reference to the hospital of Saint-
Antoine de Viennois, near the French city of Grenoble.

« 123 »

Count Roland holds his bloody sword in hand.
1630 He has heard well how the Frenchmen are dismayed;
he feels so sad, he thinks his heart will break.
"God grant you every ill," he tells the pagan.
"I'll make you pay well for the man you've killed!"
He spurs his eager horse into the fray.
They come together; one of them will pay.

« 124 »

Grandoine was both a fearless, gallant lord
and a powerful, hard-fighting man-at-arms.
He now finds Roland standing in his path,
and though he's never seen him, knows at once
1640 the haughty countenance and rugged frame,
the carriage, and the look within his eye:
he cannot help himself—he's terrified.
To no avail he tries to run away;
the count swings down with such tremendous force,
he shears away his helmet to the nasal
and slashes through his nose and mouth and teeth,
his trunk, and through his coat of jazeraint,°
his gilded saddle, both its silver bows,
and deep into the backbone of his horse.
1650 The two of them fall dead, beyond recall,
and all the men from Spain cry out in grief.
The Frenchmen say: "Our champion's fighting well!"

« 125 »

The battle is incredible and frantic:
The Frenchmen fight with vigor and chagrin,
now hacking through those wrists, those ribs, those
    spines,
those garments, down into the living flesh.
The bright blood gushes out upon green grass.
[The pagans scream: "We can't take any more!]°
Mohammed's curse upon you, Tere Majur;

1647. *jazeraint:* a variety of scale-armor.
1658. A line from V⁴ supplied by all editors.

your people are the hardest of them all."   *1660*
No man was there who did not shout: "Marsilla!
Ride quickly, king, for we must have your help!"

« 126 »

The battle is incredible and vast:
the French are fighting with their polished spears.
Could you but see such human suffering,
so many wounded, bleeding, dying men!
Face up, face down, they lie upon each other.
The Saracens can stand no more of this,
and, willy-nilly, leave the battlefield.
The Franks, with all their might, go after them. AOI   *1670*

« 127 »

Count Roland calls Olivier aside:
"You'll have to grant him this, my lord companion—
the archbishop is a very worthy knight.
None better is on earth nor under heaven;
he fights extremely well with lance and spear."
The count replies: "Let's help him, anyway,"
and at these words the Franks take up once more:
the blows are hard, the carnage hideous;
the Christians suffer very heavy losses.
Could you but see Olivier and Roland,   *1680*
still battering and slashing with their swords,
and, fighting with his spear, Archbishop Turpin!
The number that they killed can be determined;
it is written in the documents and notes:
the Chronicle° says better than four thousand.
The first four onslaughts all went well for them,
but with the fifth came sorrow and distress.
The chevaliers from France have all been killed,
except for sixty whom the Lord has spared.
They'll bring a handsome price before they die. AOI   *1690*

« 128 »

Count Roland sees the slaughter of his men.
He calls aside Olivier, his comrade:

1685. See v. 1443, n.

"Fair lord, dear comrade, in the name of God, what
       now?
You see what good men lie here on the ground.
We well may mourn sweet France the Beautiful,
to be deprived of barons such as these.
Oh king, my friend—if only you were here!
Olivier, my brother, what can we do?
By what means can we get this news to him?"
1700   "I have no notion," says Olivier,
       "but I'd rather die than have us vilified." AOI

« 129 »

Then Roland says: "I'll sound the oliphant,
and Charles, who's moving through the pass, will hear
       it.
I promise you the Franks will then return."
Olivier says: "That would bring great shame
and reprobation down on all your kin,
and this disgrace would last throughout their lives!
You wouldn't do a thing when I implored you,
so don't act now to win my gratitude.
1710   No courage is involved in sounding it;
already you have bloodied both your arms."
The count replies: "I've struck some lovely blows!"
       AOI

« 130 »

Then Roland says: "Our fight is getting rough:
I'll sound my horn—King Charles is sure to hear it."
Olivier says: "That would not be knightly.
You didn't deign to, comrade, when I asked you,
and were the king here now, we'd be unharmed.
The men out yonder shouldn't take the blame."
Olivier says: "By this beard of mine,
if I should see my lovely sister Alde,
1720   then *you* shall never lie in her embrace." AOI

« 131 »

Then Roland says: "You're angry with me—why?"
And he replies: "Companion, you're to blame,

for bravery in no sense is bravado,
and prudence is worth more than recklessness.
Those French are dead because of your caprice;
King Charles will have our services no more.
My lord would be here now, if you'd believed me,
and we'd have put an end to this affray;
Marsilla would be dead or taken captive.   *1730*
But we were doomed to see your prowess, Roland;
now Charlemagne will get no help from us
(there'll be no man like him until God judges)
and you shall die, and France shall be disgraced.
Today our loyal comradeship will end:
before the evening falls we'll part in grief." AOI

« 132 »

The archbishop overhears them quarreling:
he rakes his horse with spurs of beaten gold,
comes over, and begins to reprimand them:
"Lord Roland, you too, Lord Olivier,   *1740*
I beg of you, for God's sake do not quarrel!
A horn blast cannot save us any more,
but nonetheless it would be well to sound it;
the king will come, and then he can avenge us—
the men from Spain will not depart in joy.
Our Frenchmen will dismount here, and on foot
they'll come upon us, dead and hacked to pieces,
and lift us up in coffins onto pack-mules,
and weep for us in pity and in grief.
They'll bury us beneath the aisles of churches,   *1750*
where wolves and pigs and dogs won't gnaw on us."
"You've spoken very well, sire," answers Roland.
   AOI

« 133 »

Count Roland brought the horn up to his mouth:
he sets it firmly, blows with all his might.
The peaks are high, the horn's voice carries far;
they hear it echo thirty leagues away.
Charles hears it, too, and all his company:
the king says then: "Our men are in a fight."

And Ganelon replies contentiously:
1760 "Had someone else said that, he'd seem a liar." AOI

« 134 »

Count Roland, racked with agony and pain
and great chagrin, now sounds his ivory horn:
bright blood leaps in a torrent from his mouth:
the temple has been ruptured in his brain.
The horn he holds emits a piercing blast:
Charles hears it as he crosses through the pass;
Duke Naimes has heard it, too; the Franks give ear.
The king announces: "I hear Roland's horn!
He'd never sound it if he weren't embattled."
1770 Says Ganelon: "There isn't any battle!
You're getting old, your hair is streaked and white;
such speeches make you sound just like a child.
You're well aware of Roland's great conceit;
it's strange that God has suffered him so long.
Without your orders he once captured Noples:
the Saracens inside came riding out
and then engaged that worthy vassal Roland,
who later flushed the gory field with water—
he did all this to keep it out of sight.
1780 He'll blow that horn all day for just one hare.
He's showing off today before his peers—
no army under heaven dares to fight him.
So keep on riding!—Why do you stop here?
For Tere Majur lies far ahead of us." AOI

« 135 »

Count Roland's mouth is filling up with blood;
the temple has been ruptured in his brain.
In grief and pain he sounds the oliphant;
Charles hears it, and his Frenchmen listen, too.
The king says then, "That horn is long of wind."
1790 Duke Naimes replies, "The baron is attacking!
A fight is taking place, of that I'm sure.
This man who tries to stall you has betrayed them.
Take up your arms, sing out your battle cry,
and then go save your noble retinue:
you've listened long enough to Roland's plaint!"

« 136 »

The emperor has let his horns be sounded:
the French dismount, and then they arm themselves
with hauberks and with casques and gilded swords.
Their shields are trim, their lances long and stout,
their battle pennants crimson, white, and blue.   1800
The barons of the army mount their chargers
and spur them briskly, all down through the passes.
There is not one who fails to tell his neighbor:
"If we see Roland prior to his death,
we'll stand there with him, striking mighty blows."
But what's the use?—for they've delayed too long.

« 137 »

The afternoon and evening are clear:
the armor coruscates against the sun,
those casques and hauberks throw a dazzling glare,
as do those shields, ornate with painted flowers,   1810
those spears, those battle flags of gold brocade.
Impelled by rage, the emperor rides on,
together with the French, chagrined and grieved.
No man there fails to weep with bitterness,
and they are much afraid for Roland's sake.
The king has had Count Ganelon arrested,
and turns him over to his household cooks.
He tells Besgun, the leader of them all:
"Keep watch on him, like any common thug,
for he's betrayed the members of my house."   1820
He turned him over to a hundred comrades,
the best and worst together, from the kitchen.
These men plucked out his beard and his moustache,
and each one hit him four times with his fist;
they whipped him thoroughly with sticks and clubs,
and then they put a chain around his neck
and chained him up exactly like a bear;
in ridicule, they set him on a pack-horse.
They'll guard him this way until Charles returns.

« 138 »

The hills are high and shadowy and large,   1830
the valleys deep, with swiftly running streams.

The trumpets ring out to the front and rear,
all racketing reply to the oliphant.
The emperor rides on, impelled by rage,
as do the Franks, chagrined and furious:
no man among them fails to weep and mourn
and pray to God that He may safeguard Roland
until they all arrive upon the field.
Together with him there, they'll really fight.
1840 But what's the use? They cannot be of help;
they stayed too long; they can't get there in time. AOI

« 139 »

Impelled by rage, King Charles keeps riding on,
his full white beard spread out upon his byrnie.°
The Frankish barons all have used their spurs;
not one of them but bitterly regrets
that he is not beside the captain Roland,
now fighting with the Saracens from Spain,
and injured so, I fear his soul won't stay.
But, God—the sixty in his company!
1850 No king or captain has commanded better. AOI

« 140 »

Count Roland scans the mountains and the hills:
he sees so many dead French lying there,
and like a noble knight he weeps for them.
"My lords and barons, God be merciful,
deliver all your souls to Paradise
and let them lie among the blessed flowers!
I've never seen more worthy knights than you—
you all have served me long and faithfully,
and conquered such great lands for Charles's sake!
1860 The emperor has raised you, all for naught.
My land of France, how very sweet you are—
today laid waste by terrible disaster!
French lords, because of me I see you dying—
I can't reprieve you now, nor save your lives.
May God, who never lied, come to your aid!

1843. Spreading the beard out upon the chest reflected pride and
courage; tucking it under the mantle, shame and sorrow.

Olivier, I won't fail *you*, my brother;
if no one kills me, I shall die of grief.
My lord companion, let's attack once more."

« 141 »

Count Roland now goes back into the field,
with Durendal in hand, fights gallantly: 1870
he then has cut Faldrun of Pui in two,
as well as twenty-four among their best;
no man will ever want revenge so badly.
Just as the stag will run before the hounds,
the pagans break and run away from Roland.
The archbishop says: "You're doing rather well!
Such gallantry a chevalier should have,
if he's to carry arms and ride a horse.
He must be fierce and powerful in combat—
if not, he isn't worth four deniers—   1880
should be instead a monastery monk
and pray the livelong day for all our sins."
"Lay on, don't spare them!" Roland says in answer,
and at these words the Franks attack again.
The Christians suffered very heavy losses.

« 142 »

The man who knows no captives will be taken,
in such a fight puts up a stout defense:
because of this, the Franks are fierce as lions.
Now see Marsilla make a gallant show.
He sits astride the horse he calls Gaignon;   1890
he spurs him briskly, then attacks Bevon
(this man was lord of Beaune° and of Dijon°).
He breaks his shield and smashes through his hauberk
and drops him dead without a *coup de grâce*.
And then he killed Ivon and Ivorie,
together with Gerard of Roussillon.
Count Roland isn't very far away;
he tells the pagan: "May the Lord God damn you!
So wrongfully you've slaughtered my companions;

1892. The cities of Beaune and Dijon lie in the heart of the wine
country southeast of Paris.

1900 before we separate, you'll take a stroke,
      and from my sword today you'll learn its name."
      He goes to strike him with a gallant show:
      the count swings down and cuts his right hand off,
      then takes the head of Jurfaleu the Blond
      (this pagan was the son of King Marsilla).
      The pagans raise the cry: "Help us, Mohammed!
      And you, our gods, give us revenge on Charles.
      He's sent such villains to us in this land—
      they'd rather die than leave the battlefield."
1910 One tells another: "Let's get out of here!"
      And at that word a hundred thousand run.
      No matter who may call, they won't come back. AOI

« 143 »

      What difference does it make? Marsilla flees,
      but there is still his uncle, Marganice,
      who held Alfrere and Garmalie° and Carthage
      and Ethiopia, a land accursed.
      He has the black race under his command:
      their noses are quite broad, their ears are thick;
      in all, they number more than fifty thousand.
1920 These men ride up in fury and chagrin,
      then bellow out the pagan battle cry.
      "We'll all be martyred here," Count Roland says,
      "I know now we do not have long to live,
      but damn the man whose life is not sold dear!
      Lay on, my lords, and with your burnished swords
      put up a struggle for your life and death,
      so we may not humiliate sweet France!
      When Charles, my lord, arrives upon this field,
      he'll see such punishment of Saracens—
1930 for each of our dead he will find fifteen—
      that he will not withhold from us his blessing." AOI

« 144 »

      As soon as Roland sees this outlaw race,
      whose members all are blacker than is ink

      1915. Garmalie is probably the land of the Gamara, a Berber
      tribe.

and have no white about them, save their teeth,
the count says: "Now I'm absolutely sure,
beyond a doubt, that we shall die today.
Lay on, Franks! I'll attack once more for you!"
Olivier exclaims: "God damn the slowest!"
And at these words the French go wading in.

« 145 »

The pagans, when they see the French are few,   *1940*
feel proud and reassured among themselves:
"The emperor is wrong," one tells another.
Astride a sorrel horse sits Marganice;
he rakes him briskly with his golden spurs
and strikes Olivier upon the back,
lays bare the flesh beneath the shining hauberk
and shoves his lance entirely through his chest,
and then he says: "You took a mortal blow!
Great Charles should not have left you at the pass,
he's done us wrong, he has no right to boast;   *1950*
through you alone, our side is well avenged."

« 146 »

Olivier feels wounded unto death,
but gripping Halteclere, whose blade was polished,
strikes Marganice's high-peaked golden casque;
he smashes downward through fleurons and gems
and splits the skull wide open to the teeth.
He wrenches free and lets the dead man fall,
and afterward he tells him: "Damn you, pagan!
I do not say that Charles has had no loss,
but neither to your wife nor any woman   *1960*
you've seen back where you came from shall you brag
you took a denier of loot from me,
or injured me or anybody else."
Then afterward he calls for help to Roland. AOI

« 147 »

Olivier feels injured unto death,
yet he will never have his fill of vengeance:

he battles in the thick crowd like a baron,
still shearing through those shafts of spears, those
    bucklers,
and feet and wrists and shoulder-bones and ribs.
1970   Whoever saw him maiming Saracens
and piling dead men one upon the other
would be reminded of a worthy knight.
Not wanting Charles's battle cry forgotten,
he sings out in a loud, clear voice: "Monjoy!"
He calls to him his friend and peer, Count Roland:
"My lord companion, come fight here by me;
today in bitter anguish we shall part." AOI

« 148 »

Count Roland contemplates Olivier:
his face is gray and bloodless, wan and pale,
1980   and from his trunk bright blood is surging out
and dripping down in pools upon the ground.
The count says: "God, I don't know what to do.
Your valor was for naught, my lord companion—
there'll never be another one like you.
Sweet France, today you're going to be robbed
of loyal men, defeated and destroyed:
all this will do the emperor great harm."
And at this word he faints, still on his horse. AOI

« 149 »

See Roland, who has fainted on his horse,
1990   and, wounded unto death, Olivier,
his vision so impaired by loss of blood
that, whether near or far, he cannot see
enough to recognize a living man;
and so, when he encounters his companion,
he hits him on his jeweled golden casque
and splits it wide apart from crown to nasal,
but doesn't cut into his head at all.
On being struck so, Roland studied him,
then asked him in a soft and gentle voice:
2000   "My lord companion, did you mean to do that?
It's Roland, who has been your friend so long:
you gave no sign that you had challenged me."

Olivier says: "Now I hear you speak.
Since I can't see you, God keep you in sight!
I hit you, and I beg you to forgive me."
And Roland says: "I've not been hurt at all,
and here before the Lord I pardon you."
And with these words, they bowed to one another:
in friendship such as this you see them apart.

« 150 »

Olivier feels death-pangs coming on;   2010
his eyes have both rolled back into his head,
and his sight and hearing are completely gone.
Dismounting, he lies down upon the ground,
and then confesses all his sins aloud,
with both hands clasped and lifted up toward heaven.
He prays that God may grant him Paradise
and give His blessing to sweet France and Charles
and, most of all, to his companion Roland.
His heart fails; his helmet tumbles down;
his body lies outstretched upon the ground.   2020
The count is dead—he could endure no more.
The baron Roland weeps for him and mourns:
on earth you'll never hear a sadder man.

« 151 »

Now Roland, when he sees his friend is dead
and lying there face down upon the ground,
quite softly starts to say farewell to him:
"Your valor was for naught, my lord companion!
We've been together through the days and years,
and never have you wronged me, nor I you;
since you are dead, it saddens me to live."   2030
And having said these words, the marquis faints
upon his horse, whose name is Veillantif;
but his stirrups of fine gold still hold him on:
whichever way he leans, he cannot fall.

« 152 »

Before Count Roland has regained his senses
and has recovered from his fainting spell,

a great calamity descends on him:
the men from France have died—he's lost them all,
save the archbishop and Gautier of Hum,
2040 who finally has come down from the moutains;
he has been in heavy fighting with the Spaniards;
his men are dead—the pagans vanquished them.
Now racing down the hillsides willy-nilly,
he loudly calls for Roland to come help him.
"Oh noble count, courageous man, where are you?
I never was afraid with you around—
it's Gautier, who overcame Maelgut—
the nephew of old grizzle-headed Droon!
My courage once made me your favorite.
2050 My lance-shaft has been snapped, my shield is pierced,
my hauberk torn apart and stripped of mail;
my body has been run through by a lance.
I'll die soon, but I've brought a handsome price."
These final words were understood by Roland,
who spurs his horse and gallops out to him. AOI

« 153 »

Now, Roland, grown embittered in his pain,
goes slashing through the middle of the crowd:
he throws down lifeless twenty men from Spain,
while Gautier kills six, and Turpin five.
2060 The pagans say: "These men are infamous;
don't let them get away alive, my lords:
whoever fails to rush them is a traitor,
who lets them save themselves, a renegade."
So once more they renew the hue and cry;
from every side they go to the attack. AOI

« 154 »

Count Roland is a noble man-at-arms,
Gautier of Hum a splendid chevalier,
the archbishop an experienced campaigner:
no one of them will ever leave the others.
2070 Engulfed within the crowd, they cut down pagans.
A thousand Saracens get down on foot,
and forty thousand stay upon their horses:

they do not dare come closer, that I know,
but they hurl at them their javelins and spears
and darts and wigars, mizraks, and agers.°
The first barrage has killed Count Gautier;
Turpin of Reims—his shield is pierced clear through,
his helmet broken, injuring his head,
his hauberk torn apart and stripped of mail;
his body has been wounded by four spears;   2080
they kill his destrier from under him.
Great sorrow comes as the archbishop falls. AOI

« 155 »

Turpin of Reims, when he sees that he's been downed
by four spears driven deep into his body,
the brave man leaps back quickly to his feet
and looks toward Roland, then runs up to him
and says this word: "By no means am I beaten;
no loyal man gives up while still alive."
He draws Almace, his sword of polished steel;
in the crowd he strikes a thousand blows or more.   2090
Charles later on will say he spared no one—
he found about four hundred, all around him,
some only wounded, some who'd been run through,
and others who had had their heads cut off.
Thus says the *geste* and he who was afield,
the noble Giles, for whom God brought forth won-
    ders.
At the minster of Laon he wrote the charter;
whoever doesn't know that much knows little.

« 156 »

Count Roland keeps on fighting skillfully,
although his body's hot and drenched with sweat: 2100
he feels great pain and torment in his head,
since, when he blew his horn, his temple burst.
Yet he has to know if Charles is coming back:

2075. *wigars, mizraks, agers:* various kinds of throwing weapons.
2095–98. Historically there is no reason to connect Saint Giles
(Aegidius) wth Roncesvals, or suspect that he ever wrote a narrative of the battle.

he draws the ivory horn and sounds it feebly.
The emperor pulled up so he might listen:
"My lords," he says, "it's very bad for us;
today my nephew Roland will be lost.
From his horn blast I can tell he's barely living;
whoever wants to get there must ride fast.
2110 So sound your trumpets, all this army has!"
And sixty thousand of them blare so loud,
the mountains ring, the valleys echo back.
The pagans hear it, take it as no joke.
One tells another: "Now we'll have King Charles."

« 157 »

The pagans say: "The emperor's returning; AOI
just listen to the Frenchmen's trumpets blare!
If Charles comes, it will be the ruin of us—
if Roland lives, our war will start again,
and we'll have forfeited our land of Spain."
2120 About four hundred, wearing casques, assemble—
of those upon the field, they are the pick—
and launch one brutal, grim assault on Roland.
This time the count has got his work cut out. AOI

« 158 »

Count Roland, when he sees them drawing near,
becomes so strong and bold and vigilant!
As long as he's alive, he'll never yield.
He sits astride the horse called Veillantif
and rakes him briskly with his fine gold spurs
and wades into the crowd to fight them all,
2130 accompanied by Turpin, the archbishop.
One tells another: "Friend, get out of here!
We've heard the trumpets of the men from France;
now Charles, the mighty king, is coming back."

« 159 »

Count Roland never cared much for a coward
nor a swaggerer nor evil-minded man
nor a knight, if he were not a worthy vassal.

He called out then to Turpin, the archbishop:
"My lord, you are on foot and I am mounted;
for love of you I'll make my stand right here.
Together we shall take the good and bad;   2140
no mortal man shall ever make me leave you.
Today, in this assault, the Saracens
shall learn the names Almace and Durendal."
The archbishop says: "Damn him who won't fight hard!
When Charles comes back here, he'll avenge us well."

« 160 »

The pagans cry out: "We were doomed at birth;
a bitter day has dawned for us today!
We've been bereft of all our lords and peers,
the gallant Charles is coming with his host,
we hear the clear-voiced trumpets of the French   2150
and the uproar of the battle cry "Monjoy."
So great is the ferocity of Roland,
no mortal man will ever vanquish him;
so let us lance at him, then let him be."
They hurl at him a multitude of darts,
befeathered mizraks, wigars, lances, spears—
they burst and penetrated Roland's shield
and ripped his hauberk, shearing off its mail,
but not a one went through into his body.
They wounded Veillantif in thirty places   2160
and killed him out from underneath the count.
The pagans take flight then and let him be:
Count Roland is still there upon his feet. AOI

« 161 »

The pagans, galled and furious, take flight
and head for Spain, as fast as they can go.
Count Roland is unable to pursue them,
for he has lost his charger Veillantif
and now, despite himself, is left on foot.
He went to give Archbishop Turpin help,
unlaced his gilded helmet from his head,   2170
then pulled away his gleaming, lightweight hauberk

and cut his under-tunic all to shreds
and stuffed the strips into his gaping wounds.
This done, he took him up against his chest
and on the green grass gently laid him down.
Most softly Roland made him this request:
"Oh noble lord, if you will give me leave—
all our companions, whom we held so dear,
are dead now; we should not abandon them.
2180　I want to seek them out, identify them,
and lay them out before you, side by side."
The archbishop tells him: "Go and then return;
this field is yours, I thank God, yours and mine."

« 162 »

Now Roland leaves and walks the field alone:
he searches valleys, searches mountain slopes.
He found there Gerier, his friend Gerin,
and then he found Aton and Berenger,
and there he found Sanson and Anseïs;
he found Gerard the Old of Roussillon.
2190　The baron picked them up then, pair by pair,
and brought them every one to the archbishop
and placed them in a row before his knees.
The archbishop cannot help himself; he weeps,
then lifts his hand and makes his benediction,
and says thereafter: "Lords, you had no chance;
may God the Glorious bring all your souls
to Paradise among the blessed flowers!
My own death causes me great pain, for I
shall see the mighty emperor no more."

« 163 »

2200　Now Roland leaves, goes searching through the field:
he came upon Olivier, his comrade,
and holding him up tight against his chest
returned as best he could to the archbishop.
He laid him on a shield beside the others;
the archbishop blessed him, gave him absolution.
Then all at once despair and pain well up,
and Roland says: "Olivier, fair comrade,

you were the son of wealthy Duke Renier,
who ruled the frontier valley of Runers.
To break a lance-shaft or to pierce a shield,   *2210*
to overcome and terrify the proud,
to counsel and sustain the valorous,
to overcome and terrify the gluttons,°
no country ever had a better knight."

« 164 »

Count Roland, looking on his lifeless peers
and Olivier, whom he had cared for so,
is seized with tenderness, begins to weep.
The color has all vanished from his face;
he cannot stand, the pain is so intense;
despite himself, he falls to earth unconscious.   *2220*
The archbishop says: "Brave lord, you've come to
    grief."

« 165 »

The archbishop, upon seeing Roland faint,
feels sorrow such as he has never felt,
extends his hand and takes the ivory horn.
At Roncesvals there is a running stream;
he wants to fetch some water there for Roland;
with little, stumbling steps he turns away,
but can't go any farther—he's too weak
and has no strength, has lost far too much blood.
Before a man could walk across an acre,   *2230*
his heart fails, and he falls upon his face.
With dreadful anguish death comes over him.

« 166 »

Count Roland, now regaining consciousness,
gets on his feet, in spite of dreadful pain,
and scans the valleys, scans the mountainsides,
across the green grass, out beyond his comrades.
He sees the noble baron lying there—
the archbishop, sent by God in His own name.

2213. A line of doubtful authenticity.

Confessing all his sins, with eyes upraised
2240 and both hands clasped and lifted up toward Heaven,
he prays that God may grant him Paradise.
Now Turpin, Charles's warrior, is dead:
in mighty battles and in moving sermons
he always took the lead against the pagans.
May God bestow on him His holy blessing! AOI

« 167 »

Count Roland sees the archbishop on the ground:
he sees the entrails bulging from his body.
His brains are boiling out upon his forehead.
Upon his chest, between the collarbones,
2250 he laid crosswise his beautiful white hands,
lamenting him, as was his country's custom:
"Oh noble vassal, well-born chevalier,
I now commend you to celestial Glory.
No man will ever serve Him with such zeal;
no prophet since the days of the Apostles
so kept the laws and drew the hearts of men.
Now may your soul endure no suffering;
may Heaven's gate be opened up for you!"

« 168 »

Count Roland realizes death is near:
2260 his brains begin to ooze out through his ears.
He prays to God to summon all his peers,
and to the angel Gabriel, himself.
Eschewing blame, he takes the horn in hand
and in the other Durendal, his sword,
and farther than a crossbow fires a bolt,
heads out across a fallow field toward Spain
and climbs a rise. Beneath two lovely trees
stand four enormous marble monoliths.
Upon the green grass he has fallen backward
2270 and fainted, for his death is near at hand.

« 169 »

The hills are high, and very high the trees;
four massive blocks are there, of gleaming marble;

upon green grass Count Roland lies unconscious.
And all the while a Saracen is watching:
he lies among the others, feigning death;
he smeared his body and his face with blood.
He rises to his feet and starts to run—
a strong, courageous, handsome man he was;
through pride he enters into mortal folly—
and pinning Roland's arms against his chest,   2280
he cries out: "Charles's nephew has been vanquished;
I'll take this sword back to Arabia."
And as he pulls, the count revives somewhat.

« 170 »

Now Roland feels his sword is being taken
and, opening his eyes, he says to him:
"I know for certain you're not one of us!"
He takes the horn he didn't want to leave
and strikes him on his jeweled golden casque;
he smashes through the steel and skull and bones,
and bursting both his eyeballs from his head,   2290
he tumbles him down lifeless at his feet
and says to him: "How dared you, heathen coward,
lay hands on me, by fair means or by foul?
Whoever hears of this will think you mad.
My ivory horn is split across the bell,
and the crystals and the gold are broken off."

« 171 »

Now Roland feels his vision leaving him,
gets to his feet, exerting all his strength;
the color has all vanished from his face.
In front of him there is a dull gray stone;   2300
ten times he strikes it, bitter and dismayed:
the steel edge grates, but does not break or nick.
"Oh holy Mary, help me!" says the count,
"Oh Durendal, good sword, you've come to grief!
When I am dead, you won't be in my care.
I've won with you on many battlefields
and subjugated many spacious lands
now ruled by Charles, whose beard is shot with gray.

No man who flees another should possess you!
2310 A loyal knight has held you many years;
your equal holy France will never see."

« 172 »

Roland strikes the great carnelian° stone:
the steel edge grides, but does not break or chip.
And when he sees that he cannot destroy it,
he makes this lamentation to himself:
"Oh Durendal, how dazzling bright you are—
you blaze with light and shimmer in the sun!
King Charles was in the Vales of Moriane°
when God in Heaven had His angel tell him
2320 that he should give you to a captain-count:
the great and noble king then girded me.
With this I won Anjou and Brittany,°
and then I won him both Poitou and Maine,
with this I won him Normandy the Proud,
and then I won Provence and Aquitaine,
and Lombardy, as well as all Romagna.
With this I won Bavaria, all Flanders,
and Burgundy, the Poliani lands,
Constantinople, where they did him homage—
2330 in Saxony they do what he commands.
With this I won him Scotland, Ireland too,
and England, which he held as his demesne.
With this I've won so many lands and countries
which now are held by Charles, whose beard is white.
I'm full of pain and sorrow for this sword;
I'd rather die than leave it to the pagans.
Oh God, my Father, don't let France be shamed!"

« 173 »

Roland hammers on a dull gray stone
and breaks off more of it than I can say:

2312. *carnelian:* a flesh-red variety of quartz.
2318. The Vales of Moriane consist of three mountain valleys on
the Swiss-Italian border which made up the diocese of St. Jean
de Maurienne.
2322–32. Needless to say, historical fact has been stretched somewhat in this list of subjugated countries.

the sword grates, but it neither snaps nor splits,   2340
and only bounces back into the air.
The count, on seeing he will never break it,
laments it very softly to himself:
"Oh Durendal, so beautiful and sacred,
within your golden hilt are many relics—
Saint Peter's tooth, some of Saint Basil's blood,
some hair belonging to my lord, Saint Denis,
a remnant, too, of holy Mary's dress.
It isn't right that pagans should possess you;
you ought to be attended on by Christians.   2350
You never should be held by one who cowers!
With you I've conquered many spacious lands
now held by Charles, whose beard is streaked with
        white;
through them the emperor is rich and strong."

« 174 »

Now Roland feels death coming over him,
descending from his head down to his heart.
He goes beneath a pine tree at a run
and on the green grass stretches out, face down.
He puts his sword and ivory horn beneath him
and turns his head to face the pagan host.   2360
He did these things in order to be sure
that Charles, as well as all his men, would say:
"This noble count has died a conqueror."
Repeatedly he goes through his confession,
and for his sins he proffers God his glove. AOI

« 175 »

Now Roland is aware his time is up:
he lies upon a steep hill, facing Spain,
and with one hand he beats upon his chest:
"Oh God, against Thy power I have sinned,
because of my transgressions, great and small,   2370
committed since the hour I was born
until this day when I have been struck down!"
He lifted up his right-hand glove to God:
from Heaven angels came to him down there. AOI

« 176 »

Count Roland lay down underneath a pine,
his face turned so that it would point toward Spain:
he was caught up in the memory of things—
of many lands he'd valiantly subdued,
of sweet France, of the members of his line,
2380   of Charlemagne, his lord, who brought him up;
he cannot help but weep and sigh for these.
But he does not intend to slight himself;
confessing all his sins, he begs God's mercy:
"True Father, Who hath never told a lie,
Who resurrected Lazarus from the dead,
and Who protected Daniel from the lions,
protect the soul in me from every peril
brought on by wrongs I've done throughout my life!"
He offered up his right-hand glove to God:
2390   Saint Gabriel removed it from his hand.
And with his head inclined upon his arm,
hands clasped together, he has met his end.
Then God sent down his angel Cherubin°
and Saint Michael of the Sea and of the Peril;
together with Saint Gabriel they came
and took the count's soul into Paradise.

« 177 »

Roland is dead, his soul with God in Heaven.
The emperor arrives at Roncesvals.
There's not a single trace nor footpath there,
2400   nor ell, nor even foot of vacant ground,
on which there's not a pagan or a Frank.
"Fair nephew," Charles cries loudly, "where are you?
Where's the archbishop, and Count Olivier?
Where is Gerin, and his comrade Gerier?
Where is Aton? and where's Count Berenger?
Ivon and Ivorie, I held so dear?
What's happened to the Gascon, Engelier?
and Duke Sanson? and gallant Anseïs?

2393. Through a widespread misreading of Gen. 3:24, it was
believed that an angel named Cherubin guarded Paradise with a
flaming sword.

and where is Old Gerard of Roussillon?
—the twelve peers I permitted to remain?"   2410
But what's the use, when none of them reply?
The king says: "God! I've cause enough to grieve
that I was not here when the battle started!"
He tugs upon his beard like one enraged;
the eyes of all his noble knights shed tears,
and twenty thousand fall down in a faint.
Duke Naimes profoundly pities all of them.

« 178 »

There's not a chevalier or baron there
who fails to shed embittered tears of grief;
they mourn their sons, their brothers, and their   2420
    nephews,
together with their liege-lords and their friends;
and many fall unconscious to the ground.
Duke Naimes displayed his courage through all this,
for he was first to tell the emperor:
"Look up ahead of us, two leagues away—
along the main road you can see the dust,
so many of the pagan host are there.
So ride! Take vengeance for this massacre!"
"Oh God!" says Charles, "already they're so far!
Permit me what is mine by right and honor;   2430
they've robbed me of the flower of sweet France."
The king gives orders to Geboin, Oton,
Thibaud of Reims, and to the count Milon:
"You guard the field—the valleys and the hills.
Leave all the dead exactly as they lie,
make sure no lion or other beast comes near,
and let no groom or serving-man come near.
Prohibit any man from coming near them
till God grants our return upon this field."
In fond, soft-spoken tones these men reply: 2440
"Dear lord and rightful emperor, we'll do it!"
They keep with them a thousand chevaliers. AOI

« 179 »

The emperor has had his trumpets sounded;
then, with his mighty host, the brave lord rides.

The men from Spain have turned their backs to them;
they all ride out together in pursuit.
The king, on seeing dusk begin to fall,
dismounts upon the green grass in a field,
prostrates himself, and prays Almighty God
2450 that He will make the sun stand still for him,
hold back the night, and let the day go on.
An angel he had spoken with before
came instantly and gave him this command:
"Ride on, Charles, for the light shall not desert you.
God knows that you have lost the flower of France;
you may take vengeance on the guilty race."
And at these words, the emperor remounts. AOI

« 180 »

For Charlemagne God worked a miracle,
because the sun is standing motionless.
2460 The pagans flee, the Franks pursue them hard,
and overtake them at Val-Tenebrus.
They fight them on the run toward Saragossa;
with mighty blows they kill them as they go;
they cut them off from the main roads and the lanes.
The river Ebro lies in front of them,
a deep, swift-running, terrifying stream;
there's not a barge or boat or dromond there.
The pagans call on Termagant, their god,
and then leap in, but nothing will protect them.
2470 The men in armor are the heaviest,
and numbers of them plummet to the bottom;
the other men go floating off downstream.
The best equipped thus get their fill to drink;
they all are drowned in dreadful agony.
The Frenchmen cry out: "You were luckless, Ro-
        land!" AOI

« 181 »

As soon as Charles sees all the pagans dead
(some killed, a greater number of them drowned)
and rich spoils taken off them by his knights,
the noble king then climbs down to his feet,

prostrates himself, and offers thanks to God.   2480
When he gets up again, the sun has set.
"It's time to pitch camp," says the emperor.
"It's too late to go back to Roncesvals.
Our horses are fatigued and ridden down;
unsaddle them and then unbridle them
and turn them out to cool off in this field."
The Franks reply: "Sire, you have spoken well." AOI

« 182 »

The emperor has picked a place to camp.
The French dismount upon the open land
and pull the saddles off their destriers   2490
and take the gold-trimmed bridles from their heads,
then turn them out to graze the thick green grass;
there's nothing else that they can do for them.
The tiredest go to sleep right on the ground:
that night they post no sentinels at all.

« 183 »

The emperor has lain down in a meadow.
The brave lord sets his great lance at his head—
tonight he does not wish to be unarmed—
keeps on his shiny, saffron-yellow hauberk,
and his jeweled golden helmet, still laced up,   2500
and at his waist Joyeuse, which has no peer:
its brilliance alters thirty times a day.
We've heard a great deal spoken of the lance
with which Our Lord was wounded on the cross;
that lance's head is owned by Charles, thank God;
he had its tip inletted in the pommel.
Because of this distinction and this grace,
the name "Joyeuse" was given to the sword.
The Frankish lords will not forget this fact:
they take from it their battle cry, "Monjoy."   2510
Because of this, no race can stand against them.

« 184 »

The night is clear, the moon is radiant:
though Charles is lying down, he grieves for Roland;

Olivier weighs heavy on him, too,
as do the dozen peers and all the Frenchmen
he left in bloody death at Roncesvals.
He cannot help himself: he weeps and mourns
and prays to God their souls may be delivered.
The king is tired, for his pain is very great;
2520 he falls asleep; there's no more he can do.
Throughout the fields, the Franks are sleeping now,
nor could a single horse stay on his feet;
the ones who want grass crop it lying down.
He's learned much, who has come to know pain well.

« 185 »

Charles slumbers like a man who has been tortured.
The Lord has sent Saint Gabriel to him,
commanding him to watch the emperor;
all night the angel stands close by his head
and, in a vision sent him, prophesies
2530 a battle to be waged against his men;
foreboding images reveal its meaning.
First Charles directs his gaze up toward the sky,
perceiving thunderbolts and winds and hail
and sheets of rain and awe-inspiring storms;
then flames and fireballs mainfest themselves
and fall down suddenly on all his men.
Those spears of ash and apple catch on fire,
as do those shields, except the golden bosses;
the shafts of all those sharpened lances burst,
2540 the hauberks buckle, and those casques of steel.
He sees his chevaliers in agony:
bears and leopards come to eat them up,
along with serpents, vipers, dragons, fiends,
and griffins,° even—more than thirty thousand,
and not one fails to leap upon the French.
The Frenchmen cry out: "Help us, Charlemagne!"
The king is filled with sympathy and grief,
and tries to hurry there, but is restrained:
a mighty lion stalks him from a wood,
2550 so very baleful, furious, and proud,

2544. *griffin:* a monster, half lion and half eagle.

he singles out his person, then attacks him.
And there they grapple in each other's arms;
he can't tell which one strikes or which one falls.
The emperor has not awakened yet.

« 186 »

A second vision later comes to him:
he was in France, at Aix, upon a terrace;
he held a bear cub on a double chain,
and from the Ardennes saw thirty bears approach;
each one could speak exactly like a man.
They said to him: "Sire, give us back our own!   2560
It isn't right that he should be with you;
we have to give assistance to our kin."
A greyhound now comes bounding from his palace,
attacks the largest member of the group
on the green grass, well away from his companions.
The king observes a marvelous mêlée,
but cannot tell who wins or who does not.
And this is what God's angel showed the lord.
King Charles sleeps on until the break of day.

« 187 »

The king Marsilla fled to Saragossa,   2570
dismounted in the shadow of an olive,
and handed over sword and casque and byrnie;
he lies down wretchedly upon green grass.
His right hand has been cut completely off—
he passes out from pain and loss of blood.
In front of him his woman, Bramimonde,
is sobbing, wailing, making loud lament,
along with more than twenty thousand men,
who call down curses on sweet France and Charles.
They scurry to Apollo, in a crypt,   2580
insult him, mutilate him horribly:
"Oh evil god, why bring such shame on us?
Why *our* king you allowed to be defeated?
You give poor pay to those who serve you well!"
They take away his scepter and his crown,
then hang him from a column by the hands,

and topple it to earth about their feet.
They pound on him and shatter him with mauls.
They strip the fire-red gem off Termagant
2590 and throw Mohammed down into a ditch,
where pigs and dogs will gnaw and trample him.

« 188 »

Marsilla has recovered from his faint
and had them take him to his vaulted chamber,
whose walls are chased and painted many colors.
And Bramimonde, the queen, there weeps for him;
she tears her hair, proclaims her wretchedness,
and then she cries out in a piercing voice:
"Oh Saragossa, today you've been despoiled
of the noble king who held you as his fief!
2600 Our gods committed villainy out there
this morning, by deserting him in battle.
The great emir will prove himself a coward
unless he goes against those rugged men,
who are so proud they don't care for their lives.
The emperor whose beard is streaked with gray
has fortitude and great audacity.
He'll never run, so long as he's embattled—
too bad there's no one here to bring him down!"

« 189 »

The emperor, by dint of his great power,°
2610 has been in Spain for all of seven years,
has taken castles there, and many towns.
The king Marsilla did the best he could:
the first year he sent letters, sealed with wax,
addressed to Baligant in Babylon°
(he was emir, a very ancient man,
who had lived through Homer's time and Vergil's
         too):
this brave lord is to rescue Saragossa;

2609. The Baligant episode begins here.
2614. *Babylon:* Cairo.

if he does not, then he'll desert his gods,°
along with all those idols that he loves,
and he'll accept the holy Christian faith,   2620
and try to come to terms with Charlemagne.
This man is far away, and wastes much time.
He calls his people up from forty realms,
commands that his great dromonds be made ready,
as well as warships, barges, galleys, boats;
at a seaport down from Alexandria
he has his whole flotilla fitted out.
It is in May, the first day of the summer,
before he puts to sea with all his host.

« 190 »

The number in that devilish host is vast: 2630
they swiftly sail along and row and steer.
Upon those mastheads and those high-pitched prows
they've set out multitudes of lamps and rubies.
Up there on high, they send forth such a beam,
they make the sea more beautiful by night.
And as they come up to the Spanish coast,
the countryside, reflecting them, grows bright.
This information reaches King Marsilla. AOI

« 191 »

The pagan troops are in no mood to pause:
they leave the sea and, entering fresh waters,   2640
continue past Marbrise and then Marbrose,
their vessels all proceeding up the Ebro.
They have a multitude of lamps and rubies
providing them great brightness through the night.
When day comes, they arrive in Saragossa. AOI

« 192 »

The day is clear, the sun is radiant:
the emir has disembarked now from his barge.

2618. If he [Baligant] does not, then he [Marsilla] will desert
his gods . . ."

Espaneliz comes toward him from the right,
with a group of kings, some seventeen, in tow,
2650 and counts and dukes—I do not know how many.
Beneath a laurel, out upon a field,
they throw a white silk spread upon green grass
and place an ivory throne on top of it.
The pagan Baligant here takes his seat;
the others all remain upon their feet.
The first of them to speak out was their lord:
"Now listen to me, brave and noble knights!
King Charles, the emperor of all the Franks,
ought not to eat, unless I tell him to.
2660 He's brought me large-scale warfare all through Spain:
I'm going into sweet France after him.
As long as I'm alive, I won't give up
until he dies, or lives a recreant!"
He smacks his right-hand glove across his knee.

« 193 »

Now having said this, he will never fail,
for all the gold there is beneath the sky,
to go to Aix, where Charles holds audience.
His liege-men praise him, give him their advice;
and then he calls a couple of his knights,
2670 one Clarifan, the other Clariën:
"You both are sons of Maltraïen, the king
who used to be a willing messenger:
I order you to go to Saragossa;
advise Marsilla, on behalf of me,
that I have come to help him with the French;
there'll be a mighty battle, once I find them.
Then give him, folded up, this glove of gold—
make sure he draws it onto his right hand—
present him with this staff of beaten gold,
2680 and have him come swear fealty to me.
I'm going into France to fight with Charles:
if he will not beg mercy at my feet
and turn his back upon the Christian law,
then I shall take the crown right off his head."
The pagans answer: "Sire, you've spoken well."

« 194 »

Now Baligant says: "On your horses, barons:
one take the glove, the other one the staff."
And these men answer him: "Dear sire, we will."
They ride until they get to Saragossa:
they put ten gates behind them, cross four bridges   2690
and all the streets on which the townsmen live.
As they approach the city on the hill,
they hear a mighty clamor toward the palace:
great numbers of that heathen race are there;
they weep and cry, they manifest great sorrow,
they mourn their gods Mohammed, Termagant,
and Apollo, whom they nevermore will have.
"Wretches, what will come of us?" they say.
"Calamity has come to us today,
for we have been deprived of King Marsilla—   2700
Count Roland chopped his right hand yesterday—
nor do we still have Jurfaleu the Blond;
today all Spain will be within their grasp."
The two envoys dismount upon the terrace.

« 195 »

They leave their horses underneath an olive;
two Saracens come take them by the reins.
The messengers hold one another's cloaks,
and then go up into the lofty palace.
As soon as they are in the vaulted chamber,
with all good will they blunder in their greeting: 2710
"Mohammed, who doth hold us in his keeping,
our lord Apollo, too, and Termagant,
protect the king and keep the queen from harm!"
"Such silliness I hear!" says Bramimonde.
"These gods of ours behave like renegades.
At Roncesvals they worked malicious wonders;
they let our chevaliers be massacred,
forsook this lord of mine in the thick of battle.
His right hand's gone—he'll get no help from it—
that rich count Roland cut it off for him.   2720
All Spain will be in Charles's keeping now;

forlorn, aggrieved, what will become of me?
Alas! Will no one here put me to death?" AOI

« 196 »

Says Clariēn: "Don't talk so much, my lady;
we're envoys from the pagan Baligant,
who says Marsilla will be kept from harm,
and sends to him his gauntlet and his staff.
We have four thousand barges on the Ebro,
and lighters, sailing warships, racing galleys,
2730 and dromonds—there are more than I can say.
The emir is powerful and opulent;
he's going into France for Charlemagne,
intent on making him a corpse or convert."
Says Bramimonde: "He needn't go so far,
for you can find the Franks much nearer here;
they've sojourned in this country seven years.
The emperor's a noble fighting man;
he'd rather die than flee the battlefield;
to him each king beneath the sky's a child:
2740 King Charles does not fear any man alive."

« 197 »

"Have done with that!" the king Marsilla says.
He tells the messengers: "Address *me,* lords.
You see that death is closing in on me,
and I possess no daughter, son, or heir;
I had one—he was killed last evening.
Inform my lord that he should come to see me.
The emir has a prerogative to Spain;
if he desires it, I'll renounce my claim,
so he may keep it safe against the French!
2750 I'll tell him how to handle Charlemagne:
a month from now he'll hold him prisoner.
Present him with the keys to Saragossa,
then tell him, if he trusts me, not to leave."
And these men answer: "Sire, you've spoken truly."
AOI

« 198 »

Marsilla said then: "Charles the emperor
has killed my men for me, laid waste my land,
and violated and destroyed my cities.
Last night he lay beside the Ebro's waters—
no more than seven leagues from here, I'd say.
Tell the emir to lead his forces there;   2760
through you I send him this word: give them battle."
He handed them the keys to Saragossa,
then both the messengers bowed down to him
and, taking leave, they promptly turned to go.

« 199 »

The two envoys have climbed upon their horses.
They ride forth from the city hurriedly
and come to the emir in disarray,
presenting him the keys to Saragossa.
"Just what have you found out?" says Baligant,
"and where is King Marsilla, whom I sent for?"   2770
"He's wounded unto death," says Clarïen.
"Just yesterday the emperor had crossed
the pass—he planned to go into sweet France—
he formed a rear guard that would do him honor:
his nephew was assigned to it—Count Roland—
Olivier, and all the dozen peers,
and twenty thousand armored men from France.
The valiant King Marsilla gave them battle.
When he and Roland met upon the field,
he gave him such a blow with Durendal,   2780
it sheared his right hand cleanly from his body.
He killed his son, whom he had held so dear,
and all the barons he had taken there.
He turned and ran, for he could stand no more;
the emperor pursued him doggedly.
The king sends word for you to give him help,
and cedes to you his claim on the Spanish realm."
Thereafter Baligant begins to brood
with grief so cruel it almost drives him mad. AOI

« 200 »

2790 "My lord emir," continues Clariën,
    "in battle yesterday at Roncesvals
    both Roland and Olivier were killed;
    the dozen peers, whom Charles had held so dear,
    and twenty thousand of their Franks are dead.
    The king Marsilla lost his right hand there,
    and the emperor pursued him doggedly;
    there's not a knight remaining in this land
    who's not been killed or drowned beneath the Ebro.
    Down on its bank the French have made their camp.
2800 They've come so close to us within this land
    that if you wish, their way back will be hard."
    Now Baligant's expression grows ferocious;
    his heart is filled with pleasure and delight.
    He rises from the throne, gets to his feet,
    and then he calls out: "Barons, don't delay!
    Get off the ships, and then mount up and ride!
    If now old Charlemagne does not take flight,
    the king Marsilla soon will be avenged:
    for his right hand I'll let him have a head."

« 201 »

2810 The Arab pagans issued from the ships,
    then climbed upon their horses and their mules,
    began to ride—what else were they to do?
    The emir, once he had set them all in motion,
    calls Gemalfin, a favorite of his:
    "I'm giving you command of all my hosts."
    He got upon his sorrel destrier:
    together with four dukes, he took the lead
    and rode thus, till he got to Saragossa.
    Upon a marble terrace he dismounted;
2820 four counts were standing by to hold his stirrup.
    He climbed the flight of steps up to the palace.
    Now Bramimonde comes running up to him
    and tells him: "I've been doomed to wretchedness!
    I've lost my lord, sire, so disgracefully!"
    She sinks down at his feet; he lifts her up,
    and sadly they ascended to the chamber. AOI

« 202 »

The king Marsilla, seeing Baligant,
has called upon two Spanish Saracens:
"Hold onto me, so I may sit upright."
He has taken up a glove in his left hand,   *2830*
and now Marsilla says: "Sir king, emir,
I hereby cede my lands to you entire,
and Saragossa, with all attendant honors.
I've ruined myself and all my subjects, too."
The other answers: "I am sadder still—
but I cannot converse with you at length;
I know quite well that Charles won't wait for me,
but I shall take your glove, in any case."
He turns away to weep with bitterness, AOI
descends the stairway leading from the palace,   *2840*
climbs on his horse, and spurs back to his host.
He rides so hard, he stays out in the lead,
and as he goes, he calls out now and then:
"Come, pagans—they're already taking flight!" AOI

« 203 »

In the morning, as the dawn was just appearing,
the emperor, King Charles, awoke from sleep.
Saint Gabriel, who watches him for God,
lifts up his hand and makes His sign on him.
The king arinos, takes his armor off,
then all the others in the host disarm.   *2850*
They've mounted up, and now they ride full force
along those endless lanes, those outstretched roads,
until the horrid carnage comes in view
at Roncesvals, there where the battle was. AOI

« 204 »

King Charles has ridden into Roncesvals:
he starts to mourn for all the dead he finds.
He tells the Frenchmen: "At a walk, my lords,
for I myself shall have to go ahead,

so I may find the body of my nephew.
2860 Upon a solemn feast day once, at Aix,
my gallant chevaliers were making boasts
about stupendous fights and bold assaults—
I overheard there one thing Roland said:
he'd never die within a foreign realm
until he'd gone beyond his men and peers,
and he would have his head turned toward their land;
the lord would meet his end still conquering."
Ahead of all the rest about as far
as one can throw a stick, he climbed a rise.

« 205 »

2870 The emperor, while searching for his nephew,
finds many plants upon the field whose blooms
have been vermillioned in our barons' blood.
And overcome by pity, he must weep.
Beneath two trees he gets down off his horse;
he spots the strokes of Roland on three stones
and sees his nephew lying on green grass.
No wonder Charles is overcome by grief.
Dismounting, he goes running up to him
and takes the baron's head between his hands.
2880 By sorrow torn, he falls across him, senseless.

« 206 »

The emperor recovered from his faint.
Duke Naimes, together with Count Acelin,
Thierry, his brother Gefrey of Anjou,
take up the king and stand him by a pine.
He looks down, sees his nephew lying there,
then very softly starts to say farewell:
"Friend Roland, God be merciful to you!
No man so chivalrous has ever lived
to undertake great battles, and to end them.
2890 My honor is beginning its decline."
Charles faints away; he cannot help himself. AOI

« 207 »

King Charles has come to from his fainting spell;
four barons still support him with their hands.
He looks down, sees his nephew lying there.
The body, though well knit, has lost its flush;
the eyes, rolled back, are very deeply shaded.
Charles mourns for him in love and loyalty:
'Friend Roland, may God place your soul in flowers
in Paradise, among the glorious!
How bad a lord you followed into Spain!   2900
The day will never come that I shan't mourn you.
My confidence and power will decline—
I'll have nobody to sustain my honor.
I don't think I've a friend beneath the sky;
though I have kinsmen, there are none so brave."
He rips out handfuls of his curly hair.
A hundred thousand Franks so pity him
that there's not one of them but weeps with pain. AOI

« 208 »

"Friend Roland, I am going into France,
and when I'm in my chamber at Laon,°   2910
from many kingdoms foreigners will come,
and they'll inquire: 'Where is the captain-count?'
I'll say to them that he is dead in Spain.
In deepest sorrow I shall rule my kingdom;
the day won't come that I shan't weep and mourn.

« 209 »

"Friend Roland, gallant fighter, handsome youth:
when I am in my chapel back at Aix,
the men will come and ask to hear the news.
'Incredible and grievous,' I shall tell them.
'My nephew's dead, who won so much for me.'   2920

2910. Actually Laon (Aisne) became the Carolingian capital only
a century after Charlemagne's time, but here it shares the honors
with Aix.

The Saxons will rise up against me now,
and the Bulgars, Huns—so many devilish folk—
Apulians° and Romans and Sicilians,
and those from Africa and Califerne;°
and then my pains and troubles will begin.
Who'll lead my armies forcefully enough,
when he who always guided us is dead?
Oh France, how direly you have been diminished!
I feel so sad I do not want to live."
2930 He starts to yank upon his whitish beard
with both hands, and the hair upon his head.
A hundred thousand Franks fall down unconscious.

« 210 »

"Friend Roland, God be merciful to you!
And may your soul be brought to Paradise!
The man who killed you desolated France.
I have no wish to live, I feel so sad
for the members of my house° who died for me.
May God, the son of holy Mary, grant,
before I reach the main pass at Sizer,
2940 my soul to be dissevered from my body,
put down and settled in the midst of them,
and my flesh to be interred not far from theirs!"
His eyes shed tears, he tugs at his white beard.
"Now Charles is greatly anguished," says Duke
Naimes. AOI

« 211 »

"Sir emperor," says Gefrey of Anjou,
"do not give in so utterly to grief,
but let the field be searched for those of us
the men from Spain have killed in the engagement,
and have them taken to a common grave."
2950 Whereon the king says: "Sound your horn for this."
AOI

2923–24. Apulia is a department in southeastern Italy; the land of
Califerne lay in the area of modern Syria.
2937. *members of my house* (OF *maisnee*): See v. 1407, n.

« 212 »

Gefrey of Anjou has blown his trumpet.
The French dismount, for Charles has ordered it,
and all their friends, whom they have found dead
    there,
they took directly to a common grave.
Here gathered are a multitude of bishops,
of abbots, canons, monks, and tonsured priests;
they shrove and blessed them in the name of God;
they kindled myrrh and incense at the place,
swung censers all around them zealously,
and then with stately honor they interred them,   2960
and left them there—what else were they to do? AOI

« 213 »

The emperor has had them lay out Roland,
Olivier, and the archbishop Turpin,
and in his presence had their bodies opened.
Their hearts are gathered up in a silken cloth
and put into a gleaming marble casket.
This done, they took the bodies of the barons,
and into buckskin shrouds they put the lords,
bathed thoroughly in spices and in wine.
The king gives orders to Thibaud, Geboin,   2970
the border lord Oton, and Count Milon:
"Convey them in three wagons on the road."
They are wholly swathed in palls of Galazine.° AOI

« 214 »

As Charles the emperor prepared to go,
the vanguard of the pagans rose before him.
Two messengers emerged from those out front,
and spoke for the emir, proclaiming battle:
"Vain king, don't think that you will get away!
See Baligant, who's riding after you;
he leads a mighty army from Arabia.   2980

2973. *Galazine:* this is probably a variant spelling of *Galatin*, and
refers to Galata, a town near Constantinople where ornate silks
were made.

Today we'll see if you have vassalage." AOI
At this, King Charles, his hand upon his beard,
recalls to mind the losses and the grief;
and then, with pride surveying all his men,
he calls out in his strong and ringing voice:
"French barons, to your horses and your arms!" AOI

« 215 »

The first of all to arm, the emperor
without delay has slipped into his byrnie,
laced up his helmet, buckled on Joyeuse,
2990 whose gleam the sun itself cannot obscure,
and slung a Viterbo shield about his neck.
He takes his lance in hand and shakes the shaft,
then mounts up on his good horse Tencendur
(he won him at the ford below Marsonne
by bringing down Malpalin of Narbonne)
and slackens rein, then spurs him eagerly
and gallops, while a hundred thousand watch; AOI
he calls upon the Lord and Rome's apostle.°

« 216 »

Throughout the field the men from France dismount
3000 and arm themselves—above a hundred thousand.
They have equipment wholly to their liking:
fast horses, weapons beautifully made.
And then they mount—they have consummate skill;
if they can find a way, they mean to fight.
Their pennons flutter down upon their casques.
When Charles observes so many handsome faces,
he then remarks to Jozeran of Provence
and Naimes the duke, and Antelme of Mayence:
"A man can put his trust in knights like these:
3010 with them around, a man's a fool to fret.
If these Arabs don't back down, and keep on coming,
I mean to pay them well for Roland's death."
Duke Naimes replies: "May God permit us this." AOI

2998. *Rome's apostle:* Saint Peter.

« 217 »

Charles calls aside Rabel and Guinemant.
The king then tells them: "Lords, I order you
to take Olivier's and Roland's places;
one bear the sword, and one the oliphant—
you'll ride ahead as leaders, out in front,
accompanied by fifteen thousand Franks,
the bachelors, our most adventurous.   3020
Behind them there will be that many more,
commanded by Geboin and by Lorant."
Duke Naimes, together with Count Jozeran,
has marshaled those battalions skillfully:
if they can find a way, there'll be a carnage. AOI

« 218 »

The first battalions are composed of French:
behind these two they organize a third,
in which are vassals from Bavaria,
an estimated twenty thousand knights—
the fighting won't abate because of them.   3030
There's not a host that Charles is fonder of,
except the men from France, who conquer realms.
The Danish count Oger, the man-at-arms,
will lead them, for the company is fierce. AOI

« 219 »

Now Charles the emperor has three battalions;
and then Duke Naimes establishes the fourth,
with lords possessed of splendid vassalage—
the Alemanni, come from Germany;
the others all say they are twenty thousand.
They're well equipped with horses and with arms;   3040
on pain of death, they'll never flee from battle.
Their leader will be Herman, duke of Trace;
he'll die before displaying cowardice. AOI

« 220 »

Duke Naimes, together with Count Jozeran,
has formed the fifth battalion with the Normans;
the Franks all say they number twenty thousand.
Their arms are fine, their horses good and fast;
on pain of death, they'll not be recreants.
No people under heaven can outfight them.
B050 Old Richard is to lead them in the field:
this man will use his sharpened lance out there. AOI

« 221 »

The sixth battalion was composed of Bretons;
among them there are thirty thousand knights.
These men ride forth and make a gallant show,
with pennants furled upon their painted lances.
The liege-lord of these men is called Eudon.
He gives this word to Nevelon the count,
Thibaud of Reims, and the border lord Oton:
"You lead my troops; I give this boon to you." AOI

« 222 »

B060 The emperor has formed up six battalions,
and now Duke Naimes establishes the seventh
of Poitevins° and barons from Auvergne,
approximately forty thousand knights
with very handsome arms and splendid horses.
They muster on a flat below a hill
and then, with his right hand, Charles blesses them.
Count Jozeran and Godselme are to lead them. AOI

« 223 »

The eighth battalion Naimes has now established.
Composed of Flemings° and of Frisian° lords,

3062. *Poitevins* come from Poitou, a former province in western
France; *Auvergne* was a province in central France.
3069. *Flemings:* natives of Flanders, a medieval country located
in the area of Belgium, southwestern Holland, and northern
France; *Frisian:* pertaining to Friesland, a province in the northern
Netherlands.

it numbers over forty thousand knights.   *3070*
The fighting won't break off because of them.
The king says then: "These men will do my bidding."
Between Rembalt and Hamon of Galicia,°
they'll furnish them with gallant leadership. AOI

« 224 »

Between the two, Count Jozeran and Naimes,
they formed the ninth battalion of brave men,
Lorrainers° and the troops from Burgundy.°
By count they number fifty thousand knights
with helmets laced, appareled in their byrnies;
they carry heavy spears with stubby shafts.   *3080*
Unless the Arabs hesitate to come,
these men will give them battle, once they're chal-
     lenged.
Thierry will lead them, duke of the Argonne.° AOI

« 225 »

The lords of France make up the tenth battalion,
a hundred thousand of our finest captains,
with powerful physiques and haughty features
and whitish beards and grizzled heads of hair.
They're dressed in hauberks, double-layered byrnies,
and at their sides wear swords from France and
     Spain;
their shields are fine and gaily decorated.   *3090*
And now they've mounted up, demanding battle.
"Monjoy!" they shout; with them is Charlemagne.
The oriflamme° is carried by Lord Gefrey:

3073. *Galicia:* a kingdom in the area of southern Poland.
3077. *Lorrainers* come from the medieval country of Lorraine,
which lay in the area of eastern France and western Germany,
along the Moselle, Meuse, and Rhine rivers. The region of
Burgundy lies to the southwest of Lorraine.
3082. The *Argonne* is a wooded region on the border of France
and Luxembourg.
3093. *oriflamme:* the *aurea flammula,* golden ensign of the city of
Rome, which in actuality was sent by Pope Leo III to Charlemagne in 796.

Saint Peter's once, it then was called "Romaine";
this later was supplanted by "Monjoy." AOI

« 226 »

Dismounting from his horse, the emperor
has stretched out prone upon the lush green grass
and turned his face to meet the rising sun.
With all his heart he prays aloud to God:
3100 "True Father, keep me safe from harm today,
as Thou most certainly protected Jonah
when he was in the body of the whale,
as Thou hath saved the king of Nineveh,
and Daniel from excruciating pain
when he was down within the lions' den,
and all three children in a burning fire!
Allow Thy love to be with me today!
And grant me, in Thy mercy, if it please Thee,
the power to avenge my nephew Roland!"
3110 Now having prayed, he rises to his feet
and on his forehead makes the mighty sign.°
The king climbs on his prancing destrier,
his stirrup held by Naimes and Jozeran,
and takes in hand his shield and sharpened lance.
His build is rugged, trim, and well-proportioned,
his features clean, his bearing confident.
He rides out, seated firmly in the saddle;
from front and rear alike the trumpets sound;
the oliphant booms out above the rest.
3120 The Frenchmen weep with tenderness for Roland.

« 227 »

With easy grace the emperor rides on,
his flowing beard fanned out upon his byrnie.
For love of him, the others do the same:
a hundred thousand Franks are known by this.
They pass those hills and soaring rocky bluffs,

3111. *mighty sign:* the sign of the Cross.

those sunken glades, those harrowing ravines,
then leave behind the passes and the wastelands:
they've made their way into the Spanish march
and set up camp upon a broad plateau.
The envoys hurry back to Baligant.   *B130*
A Syrian delivers his report:
"We've had a look at arrogant King Charles.
His men are bold, they have no heart to fail him,
so arm yourself—you'll have a battle soon!"
"That's gallantry I hear!" says Baligant.
"To let my pagans know this, sound your trumpets."

« 228 »

Throughout the host they beat upon the drums
and sound those horns and brilliant clarions:
the pagans all dismount to arm themselves.
The emir does not intend to lag behind: *B140*
he dons a saffron-yellow skirted byrnie
and laces up his jeweled golden casque
and then upon his left side straps his sword.
Through vanity he's given it a name;
because he's heard them speak of Charles's sword,
[he lets his own be known as "Précieuse."]°
This then will be his war cry in the field;
he orders all his knights to sing it out.
He hangs about his neck a great, broad shield:
its boss is made of gold with crystal border,   *B150*
its shoulder strap of roundel-patterned silk.
He grasps his spear, the one he calls Maltet:
its handle was as heavy as a beam,
and its tip alone would overload a mule.
Now Baligant gets on his destrier;
at his stirrup is Marcule of Outremer.
This noble lord° is lengthy in the stride
and narrow-hipped and broad across the back;
his chest is deep and beautifully molded,
his shoulders wide, his features very clean,   *B160*
his look ferocious, and his curly head

3146. A line missing from the Oxford ms. and supplied from V⁴.
3157. *This noble lord:* Baligant.

as white as flowers in the summertime.
His valor has been proven many times.
God, what a lord, if he were but a Christian!
He spurs his horse until the bright blood flows
and brings him to a gallop, leaps a ditch
some fifty feet in width, could it be measured.
The pagans shout: "This man should hold the
        marches!
No Frenchman who may come to fight with him
3170   will fail, to die, whatever he may wish.
King Charles is crazy not to have withdrawn." AOI

« 229 »

The picture of a baron, the emir
displays a beard as white as any flower;
a man supremely learned in his law,
as well as bold and arrogant in battle.
His son Malprimes is very chivalrous,
robust and tall, the image of his forebears.
He tells his father: "Let us ride, my lord;
if we see Charles at all, I'll be surprised."
3180   Says Baligant: "Oh yes, for he is very brave—
great praise for him is found in many *gestes*—
but since his nephew Roland is no more,
he won't possess the strength to hold us off." AOI

« 230 »

"Malprimes, fair son," continues Baligant,
"just yesterday brave Roland was brought down,
along with valiant, bold Olivier,
the dozen peers, whom Charles once held so dear,
and twenty thousand fighting men from France.
I wouldn't give a glove for all the rest.
3190   Undoubtedly the emperor's returning:
the Syrian, my messenger, reported
that he has made up ten immense battalions.
The man who sounds the oliphant is brave—
his comrade's clear-voiced trumpet rackets back—
and thus they ride as leaders, up ahead,

in company with fifteen thousand Franks,
the bachelors, whom Charles has called his children.
Behind them are at least that many more.
These men will fight with lordly arrogance."
Malprimes says: "I request of you the stroke."° AOI   *3200*

« 231 »

"Malprimes," says Baligant to him, "my son,
I grant you what you've asked of me just now.
Go out at once and strike against the French.
I'll send along the Persian king Torleu
and Dapamort, another Lycian° king.
If you can blunt that overbearing pride
I'll let you have that section of my country
that lies between Cheirant° and Val Marchis."°
The other answers him: "I thank you, sire!"
and stepping forward, he accepts the gift   *3210*
(a land which once belonged to King Flurit)
at such a time that he will never see it;
nor was he ever seised° of it, nor vested.

« 232 »

The emir goes riding through that mighty host,
the massive figure of his son behind him.
King Dapamort and King Torleu together
establish quickly thirty battle corps
of chevaliers in numbers past belief;
the smallest one contains some fifty thousand.
The first is formed of men from Butentrot,°   *3220*

3200. *the stroke:* the first blow of the battle—see v. 866, n.
3205. *Lycian:* pertaining to Lycia, a province in southwestern
Asia Minor.
3208. *Cheirant* is probably Kairouan in Tunisia, a city sacred to
the Moslem world. *Val Marchis* may be the city of Marrakech in
Morocco.
3213. *seised:* a legal term meaning possessed.
3220. *Butentrot:* a valley in the Taurus Mountains, of southern
Asia Minor; its inhabitants at the time of the First Crusade were
a tribe of recreant Slavs who had renounced Christianity and had
become Moslems.

the second of big-headed men from Misnes——°
along the vertebrae all down their backs
these men have tufted bristles, just like hogs. AOI
The third is formed of Nubles and of Blos;
the fourth contains Slavonians and Bruns;°
the fifth is formed of Sorz and of Sorabi;°
the sixth contains Armenians and Moors;
in the seventh are the men from Jericho;
the eighth is formed of blacks; the ninth of Gros;
3230 and the tenth is formed of troops from strong Balide,
a race of men who never seek the Good. AOI
With all his heart, the emir now swears an oath
upon the flesh and wonders of Mohammed:
"Like a madman, Charles of France keeps riding on;
unless he turns aside, there'll be a battle,
and he shall have his golden crown no more."

« 233 »

They make up ten battalions after that.
The first is formed of ugly Canaanites
who made their way cross-country from Val Fuit;
3240 the next is formed of Turks; the third of Persians;
and the fourth is formed of Petchenegs . . .°
and the fifth is formed of Solteras and Avars°;
and the sixth of Ormaleus and of Eugiez;
and the seventh of the race of Samuel°;
the eighth of men from Bruise°; the ninth, Clavers°;

3221. *Misnes:* the Milceni from Lusatia, a realm lying in the area
of eastern Germany and Poland.
3225. *Bruns:* probably the inhabitants of Braunschweig, a province
of central Germany.
3226. *Sorabi:* a Slavonic tribe dwelling along the Elbe River in
northern Germany.
3241. *Petchenegs:* a barbarian tribe from central Asia which ter-
rorized the civilized world in the eleventh century. The remainder
of this line is unknown; the scribe made a blunder and recopied
here the end of the preceding line.
3242. *Avars:* a Caucasian tribe which ranged from the Black Sea
to the Adriatic and raided northern Italy and southern Germany.
3244. *the race of Samuel:* the Bulgarians who, led by their czar
Samuel, invaded the Roman Empire repeatedly in the tenth and
eleventh centuries.
3245. *Bruise:* probably the city of Broussa in Asia Minor, a pilgrimage site. *Clavers:* Slavs.

and the tenth of those from Occian Deserta°:
a race that does not serve Almighty God,
you'll never hear of men more infamous;
their skins are every bit as hard as iron,
and thus they have no need for casques or hauberks.   3250
In combat they are treacherous and brutal. AOI

« 234 »

The emir has drawn up ten battalions more.
The first one is of giants from Malprose;
the next of Huns, the third Hungarians;
and the fourth is formed of men from long Baldise;
and the fifth is formed of those from Val Peneuse;
and the sixth is formed of . . . Marose°;
and the seventh of the Leus and Astrimoines;
the eighth, Argoilles men; and the ninth, Clarbone;
and the tenth is formed of bearded troops from   3260
    Fronde:
a race that has no love for God at all.
The Frankish *geste* counts thirty battle corps,
a mighty force amassed where trumpets sound.
The pagans make a brave show as they ride. AOI

« 235 »

The emir, a man of vast authority,
commands that they precede him with his dragon,
the flags of Termagant and of Mohammed,
and an effigy of villainous Apollo.
Ten Canaanites go riding all around,
in high-pitched voices screaming exhortation: 3270
"Whoever wants to have our gods' protection
should pray and offer penitential psalms!"
The pagans let their heads and chins sink down

3246. *Occian Deserta:* probably the Theme of Opsicianum, a
political and military subdivision of the Byzantine Empire located
in northwestern Asia Minor.
3257. Here there is a blank space in the Oxford text, and the
other mss. have variant readings.

and tilt their shining helmets toward the earth.
The French say: "Gluttons, you are soon to die!
May utter wrack and ruin be yours today!
Oh Lord of all of us, look after Charles,
and [let us fight]° this battle in his name!" AOI

« 236 »

The emir, a man of great sagacity,
3280 now calls upon his son and both the kings:
"My lords and barons, you shall ride ahead
of my battalions; you shall lead them all,
except the finest three. These I'll hold back:
the first, the Turks; the second, Ormaleus;
and the third, the one of giants from Malprose.
The men from Occian will stay with me,
so they may go against the French and Charles.
If he will fight with me, the emperor
is sure to lose the head from off his torso,
3290 and that's the only 'justice' he shall have."

« 237 »

The hosts are large, the battle corps are handsome.
Between them there's no hill nor rise nor valley
nor woods nor brake—no place where one could hide.
They see each other clearly on the plain.
Says Baligant: "My pagan fighting men,
ride forward, seek them out, and give them battle!"
Amborre of Oluferne holds up the ensign.
The pagans bellow out its name—"Précieuse!"
"Today will be your downfall," say the French,
3300 then loudly they renew the cry "Monjoy!"
The emperor gives word to sound his trumpets
and the oliphant, which heartens all the rest.
The pagans say: "This host of Charles looks good;
we'll have a brutal, unrelenting fight." AOI

3278. *let us fight:* a reconstruction of an unintelligible place **in**
the Oxford ms.

« 238 »

The plain is broad, the country flat and open.
Light flashes off those jeweled golden casques
and off those shields and saffron-yellow byrnies
and lances with their rolled-up battle flags.
The trumpets sound, their tones are very clear;
the oliphant's high note sings out the charge. *B310*
The emir just now has called upon his brother,
Canabeus, the king of Floredée,
who rules that country clear to Val Sevrée,
and shown him the battalions of King Charles:
"Look: there's the pride of celebrated France!
The emperor is riding very fiercely;
he's with those bearded soldiers in the rear.
Across their byrnies they've thrown out their beards,
which are as white as snow on top of frost.
These men will fight with lances and with swords; *B320*
our battle will be vicious and unyielding,
a trial of arms like no one's ever seen."
Then, farther than a peeled switch can be thrown,
the emir rides out ahead of his companions
and setting an example tells them this:
"Come, pagans; I'm already on my way!"
He menacingly shook his lance's shaft
and swung its head around to point toward Charles.
   AOI

« 239 »

Now Charlemagne, on seeing the emir
and the dragon and the ensign and the flag— *B330*
the Arab forces there are so immense,
they've spread out over every bit of land
except for that the emperor is holding—
in ringing tones the king of France calls out:
"French barons, you are splendid fighting men;
you've waged so many battles in the field—
you see how vile and base these pagans are,
and all their laws aren't worth a denier.
Their army's huge, my lords, but what's the difference?

3340 Whoever will not come with me, get out!"
      At this he digs his spurs into his horse
      and causes Tencendur to make four leaps.
      The Frenchmen say: "This king's a fighting man!
      Ride on, lord—not a one of us will fail you."

                    « 240 »

      The day was clear, the sunlight radiant,
       the hosts superb, the companies immense;
      the lead battalions stand there, face to face.
      Count Guinemant, along with Count Rabel,
      both let their prancing horses' reins fall slack
3350 and spur them on. At this, the Frenchmen charge
      and go to the attack with sharpened spears. AOI

                    « 241 »

      The count Rabel is a rugged chevalier:
      he rakes his horse with spurs of finest gold
      and goes to strike Torleu, the Persian king.
      No shield nor byrnie can withstand his blow;
      he drives his gilded lance into the body
      and throws him dead upon a little bush.
      The French say: "Help us now, Almighty God!
      King Charles is in the right—we mustn't fail him."
            AOI

                    « 242 »

3360 And Guinemant accosts a Lycian king.
      He shatters his fleuron-emblazoned shield,
      and afterward he rips apart his byrnie;
      he shoves his pennant deep into the body
      and, laugh or cry who will, he drops him dead.
      And at this stroke, the men from France call out:
      "Attack them, barons, don't let up at all!
      King Charles is in the right against these [pagans,]°
      and God has left His verdict up to us." AOI

      3367. *pagans:* this word is supplied from V⁴.

« 243 »

Malprimes, who sits upon a pure white horse,
now hurls himself into the crowd of Franks,   *3370*
repeatedly goes striking mighty blows
and piling corpses one upon the other.
Before the others Baligant calls out:
"My barons, for a long time I have fed° you;
now look: my son goes seeking after Charles,
defying many knights by force of arms—
I'll never ask for any better vassal—
so take your sharpened spears and give him help!"
The pagans, moving forward at this word,
strike brutal blows; the carnage is immense.   *3380*
The fighting is incredible and heavy:
none harsher has occurred before or since. AOI

« 244 »

The hosts are large, the companies aggressive,
and all of the battalions have engaged.
The pagans fight astonishingly well.
God!—so many shafts are snapped in two
and shields destroyed and byrnies stripped of mail!
Just look at how the ground about is littered!
Upon the battlefield, the soft green grass
[is all vermillioned by the running blood.]°   *3390*
The emir encourages his retinue:
"Lay on, my lords, against this Christian race!"
The battle is extremely fierce and stubborn;
there's been none harder fought before or since.
No truce will be announced until night falls. AOI

« 245 »

The emir exhorts the members of his race:
"Strike, pagans—that's what you've come here for!
I'll make you gifts of pretty, high-born women,
and also give you honors, lands, and fiefs."
The pagans say: "For that we'll have to fight."   *3400*

3374. *fed:* OF *nurrit*, literally to nourish. See Introduction.
3390. This line, missing from the Oxford ms., is supplied from V⁴.

Attacking with full force, they lose their spears;
a hundred thousand swords and more are drawn.
Just look at all this grim, relentless slaughter:
whoever stands with them will see a battle. AOI

« 246 »

The emperor now calls upon his French:
"I hold you dear and trust you, lords and barons;
so many battles you have fought for me
and kingdoms overwhelmed and kings deposed!
I'm well aware I owe you recompense
8410 in personal assistance, lands, and wealth.
Avenge your sons, your brothers, and your heirs
who died at Roncesvals the other evening!
I know you're in the right against the pagans."
The Franks reply: "Sire, what you say is true."
Some twenty thousand men who stand nearby
swear loyalty to him in unison—
on pain of death or torture they won't fail him.
Not one of them neglects to use his lance;
before long they'll be fighting with their swords.
8420 The battle is astonishingly brutal. AOI

« 247 »

Malprimes goes riding through the battlefield,
inflicting heavy losses on the French.
Duke Naimes directs a baleful glance his way
and like a gallant fighter goes to strike him.
He splits the upper corner of his shield
and separates his hauberk's gilded skirts,
then shoves the yellow flag into his body
and piles the corpse on seven hundred others.

« 248 »

The emir's own brother, King Canabeus,
8430 has raked his charger briskly with his spurs
and drawn his sword, the point of which is crystal.
He hits Duke Naimes upon his princely casque:
one half of it is parted from the other,

the steel blade slices through five rows of laces.
His hood's not worth a denier to him;
he slices through his coif, down into flesh,
a piece of which goes falling to the ground.
The blow was powerful; it stunned the duke.
He would have fallen then, had God not helped him.
He threw his arms around his horse's neck.   *8440*
And if that pagan makes just one more pass,
the noble vassal will be dead at once.
But Charles of France is coming; he will aid him.
 AOI

« 249 »

Duke Naimes is in extremely great distress,
as hurriedly the pagan closes in.
Says Charles: "You took him to your sorrow, coward!"
With mighty vassalage he goes to strike him.
He cracks his shield and bursts it on his heart
and tears away the ventail from his hauberk
and drops him dead; his saddle is left empty.   *8450*

« 250 »

King Charlemagne is filled with great chagrin
on seeing Naimes in front of him there, wounded,
his bright blood spilling out upon green grass.
The emperor leans down and says to him:
"My fair lord Naimes, come ride along with me!
The swine who held you in distress is dead—
I put my lancehead into him just once."
The duke says: "Sire, I place my trust in you;
if I survive, you'll be repaid, and more."
Then side by side in love and trust they stand,   *8460*
together with some twenty thousand Frenchmen:
there is not one who fails to thrust and slash. AOI

« 251 »

The emir is riding through the battlefield,
and now he goes to fight Count Guinemant.

He breaks his shining shield upon his heart,
then tears away the skirting of his hauberk,
dissevering his rib-cage from his flanks,
and throws him lifeless off his prancing horse.
Thereafter he has killed Geboin, Lorant,
3470   and the liege-lord of the Norman troops, Old Richard.
The pagans then call out: "Précieuse is brave!
Attack them, lords, for here we have a champion!"
       AOI

« 252 »

If you could only see the Arab knights
and those of Occian, Argoilles, and Bascle!°
They thrust and parry deftly with their spears.
The Frenchmen, too, have no desire to run;
on one side and the other, many die.
The fighting goes on savagely till evening;
the Frankish barons suffer heavy losses:
3480   they'll have more grief before they disengage. AOI

« 253 »

The French and Arabs both fight very well;
they smash to bits those shafts and polished spears.
If you could only see those mangled shields;
if you could hear those shiny hauberks gride,
those swords° come craunching down into those
       casques;
if you could see those chevaliers unhorsed,
men screaming out, men dying on the ground—
you then might call to mind great suffering!
The fighting is extremely arduous:
3490   the emir now calls by name upon Apollo
and Termagant, upon Mohammed, too:
"Oh mighty gods of mine, I've served you long.
I'll make your effigies of solid gold, AOI

3474. *Bascle:* Scholarly opinion seems to lean toward identifying
this land as Blakia, in Thessaly.
3485. *swords:* The Oxford text, in an understandable scribal error,
says shields (*escuz*) instead of swords (*espees*).

[if only you will keep me safe from Charles."]°
Now look: before him stands his pet, Gemalfin.
The news he brings to him is bad. He says:
"Lord Baligant, the day does not go well.
Not only have you lost your son Malprimes;
Canabeus, your brother, has been killed.
A pair of Frenchmen had the lucky breaks—   *3500*
the emperor was one of them, I think—
a tall man with the look of a marquis
and with a beard as white as April flowers."
The helmet of the great emir sinks down,
and the look upon his downcast face is somber.
He felt so sad, he thought he soon would die,
then called aside Jangleu of Outremer.

« 254 »

"Jangleu, come forward," the emir begins,
"you're brave and your intelligence is great;
I've always given credence to your counsel.   *3510*
How do the French and Arabs look to you?
Are we to have success upon the field?"
And this man answers: "Baligant, you're dead.
Your gods will not protect you in the least.
King Charles is fierce, his men are valiant—
I've never seen an army so aggressive.
However, call the lords of Occian,
the Turks, Enfruns, the Arabs, and the giants:
what is to be will be—just don't delay."

« 255 »

The emir has now put out his flowing beard: *3520*
it's just as white as blossoms of the hawthorn.
Whatever happens, he will not take cover.
He sets a clear-voiced trumpet to his mouth
and sounds it clearly, so his pagans, hearing,
will rally his supporters in the field.
The Occians begin to bray and whinny;

3494. This line is supplied from V⁴.

the soldiers from Argoilles then yelp like hounds.
They charge the Franks with such unbridled fury,
burst through and part their thickest concentration,
8530 and with this single stroke kill seven thousand.

« 256 »

By no means was the count Oger a coward:
a better vassal never wore a byrnie.
When he observed the French battalions break,
he called Thierry, the duke of the Argonne,
Count Jozeran, and Gefrey of Anjou.
Then very boldly he speaks up to Charles:
"Just look at how the pagans kill your men—
may God forbid your head to wear a crown
unless you strike now, to avenge your shame!"
8540 There's no one there who says a word at this;
they ply their spurs and let their horses run
and go to fight the pagans where they find them. AOI

« 257 »

King Charlemagne is fighting very well,
as are Oger the Dane and Naimes the duke
and Gefrey of Anjou, who holds the ensign.
The Danish lord Oger is very brave:
he spurs his horse, he lets him run all out,
then goes and strikes the man who holds the dragon
until Amborre comes crashing down before him,
8550 together with the royal flag and dragon.
When Baligant observes his banner falling
and the standard of Mohammed coming down,
the emir begins to understand somewhat
that he is wrong and Charlemagne is right.
The Arab pagans [suddenly grow still.]°
The emperor now calls upon his French:
"For God's sake, barons, if you'll help me, say so!"
The Franks reply: "You didn't need to ask;
whoever doesn't fight his best be damned!" AOI

3555. *suddenly grow still:* from V⁴.

« 258 »

The day goes by and evening approaches: *8560*
the Franks and pagans battle with their swords.
The men who brought these armies here are brave,
and neither has forgot his battle cry:
the emir has thundered forth his call, "Précieuse!"
and Charles the famous battle cry "Monjoy!"
They recognized each other's loud, clear voice
and, meeting in the middle of the field,
they charged each other, traded mighty thrusts
of lances on their roundel-patterned shields.
They shattered them below those ample bosses   *8570*
and ripped away the skirting of their hauberks,
without, however, cutting into flesh.
Those cinches burst and let those saddles tip,
and both the kings land rolling on the ground,
then instantly spring back upon their feet.
Courageously they both have drawn their swords.
No longer will this combat be averted,
nor can it end until a man is dead. AOI

« 259 »

Sweet France's Charles is singularly brave;
the emir is not afraid of him or shaken.   *8580*
They let their naked swords come into view,
exchange tremendous blows upon those shields
that pierce the leather skins, two plys of wood,
and spring the nails and burst apart the bosses.
Denuded now, they hammer on their byrnies
and kindle sparks upon their shining casques.
This battle cannot ever be concluded
till one of them confesses he is wrong. AOI

« 260 »

The emir says: "Charles, consider carefully;
take counsel, then apologize to me.   *8590*
You killed my son—I know that for a fact—

and you make a wrongful claim upon my land.
Become my vassal, swear your loyalty,
then come with me and serve me in the East."
"That sounds extremely vile to me," says Charles.
"I owe no pagan either love or peace.
Accept the law that God reveals to us,
the Christian faith, and I'll soon be your friend;
then serve the King Almighty, and believe."
3600   Says Baligant: "You preach an evil sermon!"
With the swords they girded on they now attack. AOI

« 261 »

The vigorously powerful emir
strikes Charlemagne upon his bright steel casque:
it splits and comes apart upon his head—
the sword descends into his silky hair
and slices off a good hand's breadth of flesh
and instantly exposes naked bone.
Charles staggers, comes quite close to falling down,
but God does not desire him dead or vanquished.
3610   Saint Gabriel has hurried to his side
and asked: "What are you doing, mighty king?"

« 262 »

When he hears the angel's blessèd voice, King Charles
no longer is in fear or dread of death;
his mind clears and his energy returns.
With France's sword he smashes the emir:
he bursts apart the casque where jewels blaze,
then cleaves his skull—the brains come spilling out—
his face, clear down into his whitish beard,
and throws him down, a corpse beyond recall.
3620   He thunders out "Monjoy!" by way of signal,
and at this word Duke Naimes comes up to him,
holds Tencendur; the mighty king mounts up.
The pagans flee—God wills them not to stay:
the Frenchmen now have gotten what they want.

« 263 »

The pagans flee; Almighty God so wills it:
the Franks, with them the emperor, give chase.
The king now says: "My lords, avenge your griefs
and thus relieve your feelings and your hearts—
I saw your eyes shed tears this very morning."
The Franks reply: "We *have* to do it, sire."   *3630*
Each one strikes blows as heavy as he can:
of those there, very few will get away.

« 264 »

The heat is great and clouds of dust boil up:
the pagans flee and the Frenchmen harass them;
the chase goes on from here to Saragossa.
Queen Bramimonde has climbed up in her tower,
together with her clerics and her canons
of misbelief, which God has never loved.
They're not ordained, nor have their heads been
     crowned.°
On seeing the disorder of the Arabs   *3640*
she screams out shrilly: "Give us aid, Mohammed!
Oh noble king, our soldiers have been beaten,
the emir has been brought down so shamefully!"
Marsilla, hearing this, turns toward the wall;
his eyes shed bitter tears, his features sag.
While weighted down by pain, he died of grief
and yielded up his soul to lively devils. AOI

« 265 »

The pagans all have died or else [have fled,]°
and Charles has been successful in his battle,
has beaten down the gate of Saragossa;   *3650*
he knows that it is undefended now.
He takes the citadel; his troops come in

3639. *crowned* (OF *corones*): tonsured.
3648. *have fled*: supplied from V⁴.

and bed down there that night by right of conquest.
The grizzle-bearded king is filled with pride,
for Bramimonde has given him the towers—
the ten large and the fifty smaller ones.
He whom God Almighty helps fares well.

« 266 »

The day goes by, the night comes quietly;
the moon is clear, and the stars are burning bright.
3660   The emperor has taken Saragossa.
He sends a thousand Frenchmen through the town
to hunt out all the synagogues and mosques°;
with mauls of iron and axes which they carry,
they smash the effigies and all the idols;
no sorcery or magic will be left.
The king believes in God, he wants to serve Him,
and his bishops give their blessing to the waters,
then lead the pagans to the baptistry.
If any one of them opposes Charles,
3670   he'll have the man cut down or hanged or burned.
And well above a hundred thousand souls
are baptized proper Christians—save the queen,
for she is to be led captive to sweet France.
The king desires that she recant through love.

« 267 »

The night goes by, the light of day appears.
King Charles has manned the Saragossan towers.
He stationed there a thousand fighting knights;
they occupy the town for the emperor.
The king mounts up, along with all his men
3680   and Bramimonde—he takes her as his captive.
He only plans to do what's good for her.
They head for home, rejoicing and triumphant.
With lively force they take Nerbonne° in passing

3662. *synagogues and mosques:* these words are probably synonymous, both meaning rather vaguely "pagan temples."
3683. *Nerbonne:* Arbonne, a town near Biarritz.

and reach Bordeaux, the city of [renown.]°
On the altar of the noble Saint Seurin°
he sets the horn, brimful of gold mangons:
the pilgrims going there can see it still.
On broad-beamed ships he crosses the Gironde°;
thus all the way to Blaive he's brought his nephew
and Olivier, his nobly born companion,   *3690*
and the erudite, proud-spirited archbishop.
They put the lords in white sarcophagi;
the noble barons lie in Saint Romain's.°
To God and to His names° the Franks commend them.
Charles rides across the valleys and the mountains
he doesn't want to hold up short of Aix—
he rides until he sets foot on his terrace.
As soon as he is in his lofty palace
he calls his judges in by messenger:
Bavarians, Lorrainers, Frisians, Saxons,   *3700*
and Germans he calls in; then calls in Bretons,
Poitevins, Burgundians, and Normans,
together with the wisest men from France.
The trial of Ganelon will now begin.

« 268 »

The emperor has come back home from Spain,
arrived in Aix, the finest see° of France,
and climbed up to the palace, reached the hall.
Look: Alde, a lovely girl, comes up to him.
She asks the king: "Where is the captain Roland,

3684. *renown:* a conjecture—there is a blank space in the Oxford text here.
3685. *Saint Seurin:* one of the most ancient churches in Bordeaux.
3688–89. The mouth of the Gironde separates Aquitaine and Gascony. The bodies of Roland, Olivier, and Turpin are carried across the Gironde to Blaive (Blaye) for burial, because Aquitaine was under Charlemagne's control, whereas Gascony recognized only "the grace of God and the sword of the Count."
3693. *Saint Romain's:* the church at Blaye; Romain was an early French saint.
3694. *to His names:* a conventional phrase; many medieval prayers included enumeration of the names given God in Latin, Hebrew, and Greek.
3706. *see:* capital city.

3710 who promised he would take me as his wife?"
      This causes Charles to feel despair and grief:
      his eyes shed tears, he tugs at his white beard.
      "Dear sister, friend, you ask me for the dead.
      I'll give you a much nobler substitute
      in Louis°—I don't know what more to say.
      He is my son, and thus will rule my marches."
      And Alde replies: "These words seem strange to me—
      may God, his angels, and his saints forbid
      that after Roland I remain alive."
3720 Her color gone, she drops at Charles's feet,
      is dead—may God have mercy on her soul!
      The lords of France will weep and mourn for her.

« 269 »

      The end has come for Alde the Beautiful,
      although the king believes that she has fainted.
      The emperor feels pity for her, weeps,
      and takes her by the hands to lift her up;
      her head has fallen down upon her shoulder.
      When Charles observes that death has sought her out,
      he calls four countesses to him at once:
3730 they bear her body to a nunnery,
      watch over it throughout the night till dawn,
      then bury her with grace beside an altar:
      the king provided her a great endowment.° AOI

« 270 »

      The emperor has come back home to Aix:
      the traitor Ganelon, in chains of iron,
      is in the citadel, before the palace.
      The serving-men have bound him to a post,
      with buckskin thongs have tied his hands together
      and beat him thoroughly with staves and gambrels.°

3715. Louis the Pious, Charlemagne's son and successor, was not
born until 778.
3733. *endowment:* that is, for the maintenance of the burial place
and the church.
3739. *gambrels:* crooked sticks used to hang up slaughtered
animals.

He has deserved no better than he got,   *3740*
and there, in anguish, he awaits his trial.

« 271 »

It is written in the ancient chronicle
that Charles sent word to men from many lands:
at Aix they have assembled, in the chapel.
The day is holy, solemn is the feast—
some say that it was noble Saint Silvester's.°
The charges and rebuttals now begin
for Ganelon, who has committed treason.
The emperor has ordered him dragged forth. AOI

« 272 »

"My lords and barons," says King Charlemagne,   *3750*
"judge Ganelon for me with equity.
He went with me among my host to Spain,
and cost me twenty thousand of my French,
my nephew, whom you never more will see,
and courtly, valorous Olivier.
For gain he has betrayed the dozen peers."
And Ganelon says: "Damned if I shall hide it!
Since Roland took my gold and property,
I therefore planned his suffering and death;
but I'll concede to no one this was treason."   *3760*
The Franks say: "We shall now deliberate."

« 273 »

Count Ganelon stood there before the king.
His build is elegant, his color fair:
the picture of a baron, were he loyal.
He glances at the Frenchmen, all the judges,
and thirty kinsmen, there on his behalf,
then calls out loudly in a booming voice:
"You barons, hear me, for the love of God!

3746. *Saint Silvester's:* December 31.

—My lords, I went along in Charles's host
_B770_   and served him there with loyalty and love.
His nephew Roland nursed a grudge for me
and had me doomed to agony and death.
I went as envoy to the king Marsilla
and came to safety only by my wit.
I offered battle to that warrior Roland,
and Olivier, and all of their companions—
Charles heard it, as did all his noble lords.
Although I got revenge, there was no treason."
The Franks say: "We shall go deliberate."

« 274 »

_B780_   As Ganelon observes his great trial starting,
he has beside him thirty of his kin.
One man is there to whom the others listen;
he's Pinabel, from the castle of Sorence.
He knows well how to speak and state a case,
a man quite able to defend his arms.° AOI
Says Ganelon: "I'm [counting on]° you, friend,
to rescue me from death and shame today!"
Says Pinabel: "You shall be saved at once.
No Frenchmen will condemn you to be hanged,
_B790_   or else the emperor will join us two,°
and with my blade of steel I'll prove he lies."
Count Ganelon bows down before his feet.

« 275 »

Bavarians and Saxons entered council,
along with Normans, Poitevins, and French;
and there are many Germans too, and Teutons.
The vassals from Auvergne are the courtliest—
because of Pinabel they speak more softly.
"It's better we hold back," one tells another,

3785. _defend his arms:_ that is, guard against the looting of his
weapons and armor by remaining undefeated in the field.
3786. _counting on:_ a conjecture.
3790. _us two:_ Pinabel and whoever accuses Ganelon, in trial by
combat.

"dismiss the charge and then request the king
to call it quits with Ganelon this once   3800
and let him serve in loyalty and love.
Count Roland's dead; you'll not see him again,
and neither gold nor wealth will bring him back.
[Now]° no one but a fool would go to combat."
And everybody there agreed and yielded
except Thierry alone, Lord Gefrey's brother. AOI

« 276 »

The barons now return to Charlemagne
and speaking to the king say: "Sire, we pray
that you will call it quits with Ganelon—
he'll serve you then in loyalty and love—   3810
and let him live, for he's a well-born man.
[Count Roland's dead; you'll not see him again,]°   3811a
and death itself cannot return that lord,
nor will we ever get him back with wealth."
On hearing this, the king says: "You are traitors."
    AOI

« 277 »

As soon as Charles sees everyone has failed him,
his countenance and face grow quite dejected:
he thus proclaims how crushed he is by grief.
But look: before him stands a knight, Thierry,
the brother of the angevin duke Gefrey.
He has a wiry build, rawboned and spare,   3820
and black hair and a rather dark complexion;
he is neither very tall nor very short.
He courteously told the emperor:
"Fair lord and king, do not despair this way!
You know that I have always served you well;
my lineage requires I back your plea.

3804. *Now:* a conjecture.
3811a: The Oxford ms. is defective here, and most editors repeat
v. 3802 in order to furnish an antecedent for the pronouns in the
following two lines.

Though Roland may have injured Ganelon,
your service should have guaranteed his safety.
Betraying him made Ganelon a felon;
3830   he broke his oath to you and did you wrong.
For this I judge that he should hang and die
and that his corpse be thrown [out to the dogs]°
like that of any common criminal.
If he should have a kinsman to refute me,
by virtue of this sword I've girded on
I'll stand behind my judgment here and now."
The Franks reply: "You've spoken very well."

« 278 »

Pinabel has come before the king.
He is tall and brave and quick and powerful,
3840   and when he hits someone, his time is up!
He tells the king: 'Sire, this is your dispute,
so give the order for this noise to cease.
I see Thierry here, who has given judgment;
I say he lies and will contest it with him."
He proffers him his right-hand buckskin glove.
The emperor says: "I must have good pledges,"
and thirty kinsmen swear their loyalty.
The king says then: "I hereby set you free."
He puts them° under guard till right be done. AOI

« 279 »

3850   Thierry, now seeing there will be a battle,
has offered up his right-hand glove to Charles:
the emperor, as hostage,° sets him free,
then has four benches brought into the place,
where those who are to fight go take their seats.
The others deem that things are well arranged;

3832. *out to the dogs:* a conjecture; there is a blank space here in
the Oxford ms.
3849. *them:* Pinabel's thirty kinsmen.
3852. *as hostage:* Charlemagne offers himself as surety for Thierry.

Oger of Denmark tells them the procedure,
and they send out for their horses and their arms.

« 280 »

As soon as they have been equipped for battle   AOI
they make confession, are absolved and blessed;
they hear their masses, then receive communion,   *B860*
and give their churches lavish offerings.
The two of them have now returned to Charles:
they both have strapped their spurs upon their feet
and dressed themselves in strong, light, shining hau-
     berks,
secured their gleaming helmets on their heads,
and girded on their golden-hilted swords
and hung their quartered shields about their necks;
they hold in their right hands their sharpened spears.
They've climbed upon their prancing destriers.
A hundred thousand chevaliers then wept   *B870*
for Roland, and because of him, Thierry.
The Lord knows well how all of this will end.

« 281 »

Just down from Aix the plain is very broad
and here the two brave lords engaged in battle.
They both are men of pride and of great courage,
and their horses are high-spirited and fast.
They spur them briskly, let the reins go slack;
with all their force they go to strike each other.
Their shields both break and shatter into pieces,
their hauberks rip, their cinches separate,   *B880*
the bows slip loose, the saddles tumble down.
The hundred thousand men who look on weep.

« 282 »

The chevaliers are both upon the ground, AOI
but instantly they leap back to their feet.
Alert and quick and strong is Pinabel.
Without their destriers, they charge each other,

and with those swords, whose hilts are hammered
　　　　gold,
they beat and hack upon those casques of steel;
their blows are heavy, slicing through the casques.
8890 The chevaliers from France cry out in grief.
"Oh God," says Charles, "let justice shine forth here!"

« 283 »

Says Pinabel: "Thierry, take back your words!
—I'll be your man in loyalty and love
and give my wealth to you at your desire—
just reconcile the king to Ganelon!"
Thierry replies: "I needn't think it over;
I'm damned if I'll agree to that at all!
Today let God show which of us is right!" AOI

« 284 »

Thierry says: "Pinabel, you're very brave;
8900 you're tall and strong, your body is well moulded;
among your peers you're known for vassalage—
so why not bring this fighting to an end?
I'll settle things for you with Charlemagne.
To Ganelon such justice shall be rendered
that never a day shall pass without its mention."
Says Pinabel: "Almighty God forbid!
I mean to stand up for my relatives.
I won't recant for any man alive—
I'd much prefer to die than be reproved."
8910 So once again they raise their swords and hack
upon those jewel-studded golden casques,
and blazing sparks fly up into the air.
There's nothing that can make them separate,
nor can this end until a man is dead. AOI

« 285 »

Pinabel of Sorence is very brave:
he hammers on Thierry's Provence-made casque

till sparks leap up and set the grass on fire.
Presenting him the point of his steel blade,
he splits his helmet open all its length
and cuts him down the center of his face°;   3920
his right cheek is completely drenched with blood,
his hauberk ripped wide open to the waist.
The Lord has saved him from the jaws of death! AOI

« 286 »

Thierry sees he is wounded in the face—
bright blood is falling on the grassy plain—
hits Pinabel upon his smooth steel casque
and cracks it, splits it open to the nasal,
and bursts his skull, so brains come spilling out,
then wrenches free and lets him fall down dead.
With this one blow the conflict has been won.   3930
The Franks shout: "God has worked a miracle!
It's only just that Ganelon be hanged,
together with his kin who took his side." AOI

« 287 »

The moment that Thierry had won his battle,
he was approached by Charles the emperor,
accompanied by four of his lieutenants:
the lord Oger of Denmark, Naimes the duke,
Guillaume of Blaive, and Gefrey of Anjou.
The king has thrown his arms around Thierry;
he wipes his face with heavy marten furs,   3940
then puts them down; they mantle him with others.
They gently take the armor off the knight
and help him mount up on an Arab mule.
In joy and proud array they turn toward home,
arrive at Aix, dismount upon the square:
the other executions now begin.

3919–20. The Oxford scribe repeated two half-lines here; this
translation follows Stengel's reconstruction.

« 288 »

Charles calls together all his counts and dukes:
"What's your advice regarding those I've held?
They came to court on Ganelon's behalf
B950 and served as hostages for Pinabel."
The Franks reply: "Not one of them should live!"
The king commands an officer, Basbrun:
"Go hang them all upon the gallows-tree,
and by this beard, the hair of which is gray,
if one of them escapes, you're dead and done for."
The man replies: "And what else would I do?"
A hundred sergeants help him drag them off:
the number of them there they hanged was thirty.
A traitor kills himself as well as others. AOI

« 289 »

B960 The Germans and Bavarians then left,
and the Poitevins and the Bretons and the Normans.
The Franks above all others have agreed
that Ganelon should die in awesome pain.
And so they have four destriers led forward,
then tie him to them by his feet and hands.
The horses are high-spirited and fiery,
and at their heads four sergeants urge them on,
down toward a stream that runs across a field.
Now Ganelon has gone to his damnation:
B970 his ligaments are horribly distended,
and every member of his body broken;
bright blood comes spilling down upon green grass.
Thus Ganelon has died a renegade:
a man should never boast that he's a traitor.

« 290 »

The emperor, on taking his revenge,
has called upon his bishops—those from France,
and the Germans and Bavarians as well:
"I hold a high-born prisoner in my house.

She has heard so many parables and sermons,
she wants to trust in God and be a Christian.   3980
Baptize her so that God may have her soul."
They answer him: 'Now let her have godmothers,
[well-born and very open hearted ladies."]°
The crowds around the baths at Aix are great;
the queen of Spain was there to be baptized.
The name they picked for her was Juliana.
By true conviction she became a Christian.

« 291 »

The emperor, on meting out his justice
and satisfying his enormous rage,
led Bramimonde to Christianity.   3990
The day goes by, and night comes quietly:
the king has lain down in his vaulted chamber.
Saint Gabriel came down from God to say:
"Call up the armies of your empire, Charles,
for you are to invade the land of Bire
and there assist King Vivien at Imphe,
the city which the pagans have besieged;
the Christians there call out and cry for you."
The emperor had no desire to go:
the king cries: "God, how tiring is my life!"   4000
His eyes shed tears, he tugs at his white beard.

The story that Turoldus tells ends here.

3983. A conjecture; the Oxford ms. is fragmentary here.